Can true love overcome the distance?

MY THING is that I'm in love with love. Actually, I'm in love with the possibility of true love. Which could be considered a major problem. I wasn't entirely happy with any of the boys I've been with. I've always felt like something was missing. A lot of people say true love doesn't exist. But I never stopped hoping it did. I want to be swept away. I *need* to be swept away.

And now he's here.

We grab the only two seats left. For a while we just eat our ice. Avoiding what we don't want to talk about. Seth is leaving tomorrow. He starts college in two days and my junior year starts in two weeks and we'll be worlds apart.

OTHER BOOKS YOU MAY ENJOY

All I Need

Books by

SUSANE COLASANTI

All I Need

SUSANE COLASANTI

speak

An Imprint of Penguin Group (USA)

SPEAK
Published by the Penguin Group
Penguin Group (USA) LLC
375 Hudson Street
New York, New York 10014

USA * Canada * UK * Ireland * Australia
New Zealand * India * South Africa * China

penguin.com
A Penguin Random House Company

First published in the United States of America by Viking,
an imprint of Penguin Group (USA) LLC, 2013
Published by Speak, an imprint of Penguin Group (USA) LLC, 2014

THE LIBRARY OF CONGRESS HAS CATALOGED THE VIKING EDITION AS FOLLOWS:
Colasanti, Susane.
All I need / by Susane Colasanti
p. cm.
Summary: When Skye, a hopeless romantic, meets Seth, hurt by a recent break-up, at an
end-of-the-summer party they connect instantly, but their love is tested when she returns
to high school and he begins to work his way through an Ivy League college.
ISBN 978-0-670-01423-1 (hardcover)
[1. Love—Fiction. 2. Dating (Social customs)—Fiction. 3. High schools—Fiction. 4. Schools—Fiction.
5. Universities and colleges—Fiction.] I. Title.
PZ7.C6699All 2013 [Fic]—dc23 2012029900

Speak ISBN 978-0-14-242676-0

Printed in the United States of America

1 3 5 7 9 10 8 6 4 2

For Regina Hayes

*who believed in me
from the beginning*

one

Skye

bring on the night

"SOMETHING'S GOING to happen tonight," Adrienne says. "I can feel it."

It would be awesome if she was right. We've been coming to this beach party for seven years. Nothing ever happens.

When summer is shiny and new and filled with possibility, I always hope that it will be the summer when I'll meet him. The boy who will connect with me like no one else ever has. The boy who will change my life forever.

But summer is almost over. The same sadness that always overwhelms me near the end is making my heart heavy.

We walk down the steps from the boardwalk onto the beach. This annual party that my parents and their friends throw isn't exactly a party. It's more like an excuse to sit around a big seafood cookout in the pit and gorge yourself. After it gets dark, there's a bonfire where you can toast marshmallows. The rest of the time I'm making small talk with people twice my age or trying to entertain the little kids.

There are never any cute boys. But that doesn't stop me from hoping this time will be different.

"I can't believe school starts in two weeks," Adrienne groans.

"No school talk on the beach," I demand. "This is a happy place. Only happy thoughts allowed." I've been trying to avoid all the back-to-school displays in town. Whenever I'm ambushed by one of those annoying ads in a magazine, I quickly flip the page before reality sinks in. My determination to make the most of every last second of summer is fierce.

Adrienne and I head over to the crowd with our flip-flops flinging sand around. I'll find sand in everything—my bag, my drawers, even my books—way after we pack up the summer house and go back home. I'm not looking forward to the day when all the sand is gone.

My parents are sitting together on a blanket. They're staring out at the ocean, Mom leaning against Dad, still happy to be married after twenty-one years. That's all I need. To find a soul mate to share my life with. To have a love so epic it will never die.

Adrienne's little brother runs right at her. He slams into her legs. Adrienne dramatically pretends to be tackled, sprawling back on the sand with her arms splayed out. Dustin thinks this is the most hysterical thing ever.

"Come on, you rugrat," she says. "Let's go husk some corn."

Before my parents' friends start coming up to me with their boring questions, I take a minute to watch the ocean. It's all sparkly in the evening light. Diamonds of sunlight shimmer way into the distance. I stare at the horizon, trying to find the farthest sunlight diamond. Something makes me look away.

A boy is staring at me.

He's sitting on one of the logs circling the pit. I've never seen him before. I would definitely remember.

It takes me a few seconds to realize that I'm staring back at him. I can't help smiling a little.

He smiles back.

I turn away, feeling like an idiot. Maybe Adrienne was right. Maybe something really will happen tonight. Why couldn't I be rocking something sexier than my standard oversized tee/cutoffs/flip-flops look?

"Did you know *Zenyattà Mondatta* is a portmanteau?" someone says behind me. I know it's him even before I turn back around.

"What?" I say.

The boy who was staring points at my shirt.

"Oh." I look down at the vintage Police concert tee. "This is my dad's old shirt."

"Are you into the Police?"

"They're okay."

"They're *okay*? Have you heard the Police?"

"Only when my dad plays them."

"We'll have to fix that."

A zing of adrenaline shoots through me.

"Are you, like, a Police superfan?" I ask.

"They were musical geniuses," he says. "I'm into lots of eighties music. And some late-seventies stuff. That's when the best music was made. The overplayed crap everyone listens to now is meaningless."

This boy is intense. And he's striking in a way I've never really seen before. His eyes are pale green like sea glass, like you could see right into his soul. His straight, clean-cut brown hair makes me notice his eyes even more. He's about five ten with the kind of medium build I'm into. I even like what he's wearing—green Vans, cargos, and a plain white T-shirt.

"I'm Seth," he says.

"I'm Skye."

"Do you live around here?"

"Just for the summers. Our house is up there." I point to the hill where my house sits next door to Adrienne's. Adrienne and I met the summer my parents bought our house when we were both nine. I couldn't believe how lucky I was to have a summer friend the same exact age right next door. People even say we look like sisters. Which is an exaggeration. We both have long, wavy, honey-blonde hair, but mine's darker. And our eyes are different shades of blue. Still, I think of Adrienne as my summer sister. "What about you?"

"Oh, I'm . . . staying with my dad."

When Seth takes a drink from his Coke bottle, I notice his friendship bracelets. He has a bunch of them in all different patterns and colors. His watch is one of those big ones with an extra-wide band. It looks really good with the friendship bracelets.

"I love your friendship bracelets," I say. Then I brace myself for Seth to tell me that his girlfriend made them.

"Thanks. My cousin Jade made these at camp. She sends me new ones every summer."

That. Is adorable.

"Wait," I say, remembering. "What's a . . . portmanteau?"

"A blend of other words. I forget which words went into *Zenyatta Mondatta*. Pretty sure *Zen* was one of them."

It's so weird that Seth just said Zen. Adrienne and I were talking about her new feng shui book on the way here. She wants to redecorate her room with pairs of things against the southern wall. That's supposed to bring love into your life. I totally forgot about Adrienne until now. We're the only people we actually want to hang out with at this thing. She must be ready to kill me. But when my eyes find hers in the crowd and I give her an apologetic look, it's clear she's stoked that I'm talking to Seth. She gives me a thumbs-up, then points at me "get it, girl" style. I hope she meets someone tonight, too.

This annoying lady who has the most outrageous estate on the hill swoops in to air-kiss a mom trying to get her two little kids to stop running around her in circles.

"Celia!" Annoying Lady shrieks. "How *are* you?"

"A bit frazzled at the moment," Celia says, pointing out the obvious.

"We *must* do lunch before you leave. It's been ages."

"Well, I'm not really available for lunch these days."

"Why's that?" Annoying Lady looks confused. Like the thought that a mom could be raising her kids without a nanny never occurred to her.

Seth moves closer to me. "Why do people always do that?" he says.

"Pretend not to live in reality with the rest of us?"

"That. And ask how you are when they have no interest in hearing it."

"I know," I say. "It's like people are afraid to be real." Even as I'm saying it, I know Seth is different.

I already know he's the real thing.

two

Seth

only in dreams could it be this way

I DIDN'T want to come to this beach cookout thing. I'd rather be hiding out back at my dad's.

But then I see her.

She's coming down the steps from the boardwalk with another girl. I can't take my eyes off her. Which is weird, considering that exactly zero girls have caught my attention since my heart was ripped out, stomped on, and shoved back in my chest with dirt and twigs stuck all over it. But this girl . . . Do I know her from somewhere? I feel like I've met her before. And not just because she's beautiful. If you could turn summer into a girl, she's how it would look. Shiny blonde hair. Cute cutoff shorts. Tan from chilling at the beach all summer.

Dude. She's wearing a Police tour shirt.

A part of me that's been comatose since my heart was destroyed wakes up.

When she looks at me with those unreal sky-blue eyes, I know that everything is about to change.

Nick snaps his fingers in front of my face. "She's hot," he confirms. "But she must be crazy. She obviously wants you."

My dad went to high school with Nick's dad. They grew up in Stirling, a town in New Jersey not too far from West Orange, where I'm from. I met Nick when we went over to his place for dinner a few days ago. His house is one of those massive McMansions way up on the hill. Sea Bright has an interesting socioeconomic diversity dynamic. There are all these extravagant houses up on the hill, not that far from a bunch of ramshackle beach houses down below. As if the delineation of wealth weren't painfully clear enough, a stream divides the two areas. Most of the beach houses down here look like they'd be reduced to a clattering pile of boards in a strong wind. The hill houses are oriented so that their enormous windows provide sweet views of the ocean. Their picture windows look like faces in a movie theater, all turned toward the screen.

Nick is okay. I feel like less of a loser having someone to hang out with on the beach and stuff. Nick's the one who told me about this party. I didn't have anything better to do. So here I am.

With her.

I have to know who she is.

"Go for it, man," Nick encourages when I get up. Like I even remotely have a chance. But I can't help it. My body and mind are in throwdown mode. Logic is not winning this battle.

I can't believe I'm doing this.

I walk over to her in a trance. Words come out of my mouth. I have no idea what they are, but she's talking back. We're apparently having some sort of conversation.

She says her name is Skye. When she points out that one of those gigantic houses on the hill is hers, I do not point out my dad's ramshackle hut.

"Want to go for a walk?" I blurt. I need to get out of here. I don't want her to see how awkward I am around people with money. This party seems to be all hill people. Including the shrill lady next to us who won't shut up.

"Absolutely," Skye says.

We walk along the ocean's edge. Skye takes her flip-flops off and holds them so she can walk in the water. I try not to stare at her legs.

"The moon is so pretty," she says. "Look how it's right next to that star."

"That's actually Venus."

"It is?"

"Yeah. It's brighter than any star we can see right now. And the moon's a waxing gibbous. A quality phase. But my favorite phase is waning crescent."

"Why?"

"It looks like the moons we drew in elementary school." If only I could go back. Not crazy far back to elementary school. Just back to last year. I wish I could start over again knowing what I know now. I never would have given Chloe that stuffed bear for Valentine's Day. He looked so innocent at the time with his fluffy white fur and satin red bow. But he was an instigator. An evil, fluffy instigator.

"Sometimes I miss how simple life used to be," Skye says.

"Totally. When did everything get so complicated?"

"I know, right? The highlight of my day was playing cat's cradle with my friends at recess. Now it's like some days I can't even breathe."

"Most days I have to remind myself to breathe."

"Why?"

"I'm kind of neurotic. A common affliction among artists."

"You're an artist?"

"More like a wannabe artist. I mostly mess around with mixed-media collages."

"Like layering papers and metals and things?"

"Exactly. And I like using found objects."

Skye bends down and picks up a smooth, white rock. "Here's a found object." She holds it out to me. "What can you do with it?"

"So many things," I say, despite not being able to think of even one. Skye puts the rock in my hand, her fingers brushing against mine. Her skin is incredibly soft. "Um. Isn't cat's cradle that game with the string?"

"You've never played?"

"Guys aren't really into string games."

"Anyone wearing friendship bracelets would like cat's cradle."

"Got any string on you?"

"Next time."

So there's going to be a next time?

"Old-school stuff rules," Skye declares. "I hate how everyone's stuck in front of screens all the time. It's like people don't want to interact with the real world anymore."

That bothers me, too. How does this girl know everything?

"Have you seen that sand-painting guy?" I ask. I found him yesterday on my way to the snowball place. He creates incredible designs on the concrete ramp using colored sand.

"Yes! He's amazing. His colors are so vivid."

"I know. At first I thought he was mostly using pastels—"

"—but it's all colored sand! I have a thing for colored sand."

"Me too. It works really well on collages."

We smile at each other, bonded by art.

The art of collage has always appealed to me. When I was seven, my mom took me to an exhibition at the Guggenheim with these large-scale collages. I was in complete awe. I remember winding down the spiral path, stopping in front of each piece to gawk up at it. Every collage tells a story in such a unique way. They're like pieces of a puzzle or chapters in a book. They can be subtle and speak volumes at the same time. I love how the final effect is greater than the sum of its parts.

"Guess you've been to the snowball place," I say.

"Uh, you mean my second home?" Skye reaches down to pick up a ridged white shell with gray stripes. "We've been coming here every summer for the past seven years. Snow-balls were an immediate addiction. And they're essential when it's hot. I always get them when I'm laying out."

I hope Skye doesn't ask me why I'm in Sea Bright. Escaping with her like this is making me feel alive. I can recognize parts of myself I haven't seen all summer. But talking about school would force me to relive it all over again. My friends have been telling me to get back out there. To start meeting new people. I thought hiding out in my room all summer was a better idea. Which is why my mom made me come here for the week before college starts. So I'm staying with my dad at our beach house. Except ever since he bailed last year, it's been his all-year house. That's how badly he needed to escape.

Skye stops to look out at the ocean. Standing here with her, I'm overwhelmed with possibility. Maybe I really can have the life I want someday. Even though my heart keeps telling me I can't.

"I love it here," Skye says.

"I brought my sketchbook down here the other day and worked on a new collage. This whole peaceful vibe thing is really inspiring." That collage turned out to be one of my favorites. I layered tissue paper shreds in different shades of blue and green to create an ocean look. Watching the colors of the water change over a few hours was something I'd never done before. It gave me a new appreciation for the ocean.

Skye gives me a strange look.

"What?" I say.

"Nothing." We start walking again. "Just . . . you're kind of perfect."

"Not even close. Everyone has their thing."

"What thing?"

"Everyone comes with baggage. No one is perfect. You can work on one problem, but even if you solve it there's always going to be another problem. So your 'thing' is your biggest problem at any given time."

"That is so true."

"What's yours?"

"My thing?"

I nod.

"It's a secret," she says. "Waiting to be revealed."

"Then I guess you'll have to discover mine, too."

"But I can tell you a different secret."

"Go for it."

"You know that creepy rabbit from *Donnie Darko*?"

"Yes!"

"Sometimes I have nightmares about him."

"Dude. He's *so* creepy."

"He redefines creepy."

"I looked up *creepy* in the dictionary and there was a picture of him."

Skye laughs.

There's something about this light before sunset that captivates me. Trying to re-create the colors of the water and sky isn't easy. But I keep taking mental pictures, hoping that I'll get it right eventually.

"Pink clouds," Skye says. She looks so beautiful, backlit by the sun. I didn't notice all the hues of gold and copper in her hair before.

"Race you to the dune," she challenges.

"Wha—"

"Go!"

Skye takes off running toward a big sand dune surrounded by tall sea grass. I run after her. She's pretty fast. I'm not the spontaneous type, but I make an effort to catch up with her to pretend I am. By the time I get to the top of the dune, I'm panting. I should be in better shape. I *look* like I'm in better shape. It's deceiving.

Skye laughs and twirls around. The breeze blows her hair back. The sound of her laughter blends with ocean waves crashing.

I realize we walked a long way. The party is this tiny point in the distance. We probably should turn back soon.

But for now, it's just us. Our instant connection is undeniable. I watch Skye watching the sunset colors glowing on the water.

There might never be another chance like this again.

When Skye turns to me, I don't think. I pull her close to me.

And I kiss her.

three

Skye

sweet days of summer

HOW IS it possible to feel like you've known someone your whole life when you just met him yesterday?

The way I feel when I'm with Seth is how I've always wanted to feel with a boy. That dizzy, can't-think-about-anything-else butterflies sensation that sweeps you away and changes you forever. The kind of crazy romantic movie love you always hoped was real. The kind of love you wish for your whole life and then, before you know it, it's already happening.

I can't stop smiling when I'm with Seth. I can't stop wanting to touch him. And that kiss . . .

I've heard that when you meet a soul mate, you have an instant connection right from the start. Which is exactly what I have with Seth. I know how crazy that sounds. We just met. Yeah, we've already kissed, but I'm sure Seth was just overcome by the magic of last night the same way I was. He hasn't even tried to hold my hand today and we've been hanging out for a while.

When Seth asked me what my thing was, this is what I

couldn't tell him: My thing is that I'm in love with love. Actually, I'm in love with the possibility of true love. Which could be considered a major problem. I wasn't entirely happy with any of the boys I've been with. I've always felt like something was missing. A lot of people say true love doesn't exist. But I never stopped hoping it did. I want to be swept away. I *need* to be swept away.

And now he's here.

"What kind are you getting?" Seth asks.

"Hmm?" I try to pull out of my love haze. It's not easy.

Seth points to the flavor board at the front of the snowball place. Everyone just calls it the "snowball place," but we're technically at Cold as Ice. Their sugar packets are adorable. They say COLD AS ICE with a smiling snowball.

"I'm getting spearmint lemonade," he says.

"Ooh, that's an excellent combo!"

"I try."

"I'm getting watermelon tangerine."

"Have you tried them all?"

"What do you think?" I lean closer to him so our arms touch. How he wears his little cousin's friendship bracelets is so freaking cute. I should really calm down the hormones before I scare him off completely. But I can't help it. It's like I have to touch him or I'll die. It takes an enormous effort to pull my arm away.

"I think you're a snowball fiend," Seth decides.

"See how well you know me already?"

We move up in line. My arm longs to touch his arm again.

"What's the difference between a snowball and a snow cone?" Seth asks.

"Snow cones have coarser ice. Snowball ice is smoother."

"Like Italian ice?"

"Not that smooth."

"You know a lot about ice."

"Doesn't everyone?"

Seth laughs. We order our snowballs. He insists on treating.

"Then I'll treat next time," I say. Because of course there will be a next time.

The place is packed. It's always packed when it's broiling out. We grab the only two seats left. For a while we just eat our ice. Avoiding what we don't want to talk about. Seth is leaving tomorrow. He starts college in two days and my junior year starts in two weeks and we'll be worlds apart. And I don't even know where he's going.

"So where are you going to college?" I ask.

"This might sound weird," he says, "but could we ignore all that post-summer harsh reality for now? This is the first time I've been happy all summer. I just want to escape for a little longer. I mean, if you're okay with that."

"Totally." He's right. This is so much better. We're transcending all of the everyday noise. If anyone understands about extending summer for as long as possible, it's me. It's like we're in our own world where we make the rules and nothing can bring us down. But I'm wondering why he wasn't happy before.

Seth looks at me. "I like escaping with you," he says.

"I like escaping with you, too."

He's still looking at me. Is he going to kiss me again? *Please let him kiss me again.*

"Your tongue is red," he informs me.

"Yours is green."

"We're the ones that look like Christmas."

I nod.

"Hey, you," he says.

"Hey."

"No, it's from that Cure song. 'Hey You!'"

"Oh."

"They mention Christmas in a few songs. 'A Christmas card in sepia' from 'Strange Attraction.' 'Laughing at the Christmas lights' from 'Let's Go to Bed.'"

I bite my lip.

"Yeah, we need to get you acquainted with eighties music."

"Some guy once told me it's the best."

"Sounds like he has good taste."

"Oh, he does."

"Let's roll."

"Where to?"

"Where we can literally roll."

"The rink?"

"You know you want to."

"Sweet!" The roller rink is so much fun. I've been there a bunch of times. It's kind of run-down, but it's retro in the best possible way. It has a major eighties vibe. There are posters of old shows like *The Cosby Show*, *Family Ties*, *Growing Pains*, and *Punky Brewster*. Smurfs are jumbled on the ledge behind the bar. There's a Garfield garbage can in the bathroom. Pac-Man and Asteroids video games line the wall. They only play eighties music, which I guess is why Seth wants to go. Unless he's just into roller skating. Which would make me like him even more.

You can see the rink's neon sign from way down the boardwalk. WHEEL IN THE SKY glows in bright purple neon. A pair of roller skates with hot-pink wheels dangles from the S, their lime-green laces tied to the bottom of it.

Out of all the cool relics at the rink, the best one is the old-school photo booth. Adrienne and I take a couple strips of us each year. She has hers tacked to her bulletin board. I always put our most recent photo strip up in my locker when school starts. The rest are in a special box back home. Whenever I open the box, I'm transported right back to summer.

"Shall we?" Seth says in front of the photo booth. He whisks the curtain aside and waves me in.

I scrunch over on the little bench. Seth pulls the curtain closed behind him. He presses up against me.

"Sorry, am I squooshing you?" he says.

"No, I'm good." He is so squooshing. I am so loving it.

"Should we do the same expressions?"

"Let's just see what happens."

"Game on."

Right before the first flash pops, I catch Seth checking out my expression in our reflection in the glass. He does this for the next two shots. When the photo strip comes out, I see that he matched my expression for the first three shots. We're exaggerated serious in the first one. Cross-eyed in the second. Laughing in the third. In the fourth one, I'm doing a kissy face and he's scratching his head like he's confused.

Seth rips the strip in half.

"What are you doing?"

"Pick your half." He holds the pieces out for me to choose. I take the laughing/kissy/confused half.

We get our skates and go over to sit on one of the benches circling the rink. The rink is a hardwood circle with a smaller carpeted circle in the middle. I learned how to roller-skate on the carpeted part my first summer here. It took me a while to find my balance. I kept zooming out onto the main part before I was ready. Which is why I kept falling on my butt. It would be awesome if I had that falling-on-my-butt problem worked out by now.

"Ready?" Seth asks.

"Ready." I stand up, wobbling a little.

We hit the hardwood. It always feels like my wheels are going to fly out from under me when I first start skating. But I get the hang of it after a few minutes. Seth is really good. He even skates backward. I've never been able to pull that off.

A new song comes on. Seth goes ballistic.

"This is my *jam!*" he yells over the music.

"What is it?" I yell back.

"'Perfect Way.' Scritti Politti. Please tell me you've heard this before."

I shake my head.

"You're killing me!" Seth fake stabs his heart. He does a few spirals as if he's falling to a slow, painful death.

We whip around the rink. There are only a few other people here, which is a total invitation to zigzag between them. An epic song comes on. It's "Take It on the Run" by REO Speedwagon. I'm so excited to not only recognize a song but have one come on that I love.

"I love this song!" I yell.

"You know REO?" Seth yells back.

"Of course!" Before I can stop myself, I'm busting out with cheesy hand motions to go with the song. Seth cracks up when I attempt the guitar solo on one skate. We're going too fast for me to be skating on one skate.

Just like all those times before, I fall flat on my butt.

four

Seth

back to the basics for you

I REACH down to help Skye up. I've been dying to touch her all day. The adorable way she just fell is a perfect opportunity.

"You okay?" I ask.

Skye reaches for my hand. I pull her up. When she wobbles on her skates, I put my arms around her. She presses up against me.

"I'm okay," she says.

It takes me a minute to let her go. I wanted to hold her hand when we were walking around before. And at the snowball place I really wanted to kiss her, to taste her sweet tangerine lips on mine.

But I have to chill.

If I touch her and kiss her like I want to, I will be in it again. I cannot go there. This might be the last time we even see each other. I'm amazed my dysfunctional heart is still beating after the stomping it endured. At graduation.

By a girl who said she loved me. Who dumps her boyfriend at graduation?

Oh, wait. My ex-girlfriend does.

Turns out Chloe had a whole graduation speech prepared just for me. She didn't want us to be tied down at college. It would be too painful to only see me a few times a year. She even whipped out the classic long-distance-relationships-never-work excuse. To make things even more surreal, she dumped all this on me while we were in our caps and gowns before the ceremony. We were in the gym with the rest of our class, waiting to file out onto the football field. At least she pulled me over to a corner to break up with me. But everyone could tell what was happening. In the space of five minutes, Chloe annihilated everything we were. Everything we could have been.

I took a chance on giving her that bear for Valentine's Day. The second I saw it, I knew she would love it. I knew I had to finally show her I liked her. The bear was a sign that it was time to stop being afraid. Chloe said yes when I asked her out. Everything was going smoothly. I never imagined we would crash and burn.

This was supposed to be the best summer ever. My last summer of freedom. Instead, I wasted most of it moping around the house. Not wanting to go anywhere. Not wanting to do anything.

But now Skye is grabbing my hand. We're pushing off

on our skates. She's flying even faster than before. And she knows "Take It on the Run."

Things are looking up.

When we're all skated out and sitting on the side, a group of girls having a birthday party skates by. One of the girls is throwing confetti at her friends. Some of it lands on us. Skye looks like she's five, smiling all big as she squeals at the confetti. She scoops some of it off the bench and puts it in her pocket. I'm not surprised she wants to keep some. The confetti is sparkly. Skye seems like a girl who digs sparkly things.

I make a mental note to do something with confetti in a future collage. Maybe I'll make one for Skye.

"Bye, photo booth," Skye tells the photo booth on our way out. "Until we meet again."

"Have you been to Red Bank?"

"Yeah."

"That town is trying too hard. People keep saying how arty and cool it is. I'm like, yeah, if your definition of *arty* is contrived coffeehouses and chain stores. But there's this one store with another vintage photo booth."

"Anywhere with a vintage photo booth rules."

"They also have worry dolls."

"I love worry dolls!"

"Of course you do."

Holding the door open for Skye, I wave to the guy behind the counter. Skye doesn't notice. Which is a good thing. The guy behind the counter is my dad. Who wasn't supposed to be here until later. I almost skated into the couple in front of us when I saw him come in. Skye thought I was just getting us drinks, but I snuck over to my dad and asked him to ignore us. I don't want Skye to know he owns the rink. Dad's cool with giving me privacy when girls are involved. He's been getting cooler lately in general. All he wears now are the threadbare T-shirts and ripped jeans I saw him wearing in pictures from college. Plus he's talking about getting a motorcycle. I even saw travel catalogs in his room for places like Iceland and Australia.

Skye clearly loves it here. I knew she would, which is why we came. I'm sure she'd want to meet my dad. But it's kind of embarrassing how hardcore old-school this place is. Unrenovated. Falling apart. The ceiling leaks in a downpour. One look at the enormous houses on the hill told me that this girl is used to the finer things. She expects a certain level of elegance. It's one thing for her to have fun at the rink. Discovering it belongs to my dad might be a turn-off. Her dad's probably one of those world-renowned doctors who's impossible to get an appointment with. As long as Skye is helping me escape, I want to be the guy who can bring it on her level.

Today has been amazing. It's refreshing to hang out with someone who doesn't know me as The Boy Who Got Dumped at Graduation. All that anguish evaporates when I'm with Skye. If I introduced her to my dad, I'd be taking one step closer to letting her in.

Cannot. Go there.

As we walk along the boardwalk, I debate whether or not to hold Skye's hand. She suddenly stops in front of a game stand. It's that weird one where you have to spray water in the clowns' mouths.

She sighs dramatically. "I heart him."

"Who?"

"Him." She points to the row of stuffed animals hanging above the clowns. "The purple unicorn."

"Should we try to win him?"

"He is elusive. I've tried a bunch of times. But I have horrible aim. I'd try again, but I actually have to go."

My heart drops. I was hoping we could hang out some more tonight.

"There's this stupid dinner party my parents throw every year," she explains. "I'm like required to be there."

"Sounds like a rager."

"Oh, it's some wild times. The neighbors invade our house to rant about the lack of quality cleaning ladies and brag about where they'll be wintering."

"Scintillating conversation."

"But you can meet up tomorrow morning before you leave, right?"

"Totally. Should we meet at the seagull at nine?" The seagull is this seagull statue back where the boardwalk starts. It's where we met up today.

"Okay."

I'm trying not to think about what happens after tomorrow. After we say goodbye. I'm going to give Skye my contact info tomorrow. Hopefully, she'll give me hers.

Skye hugs me. I hug her back. I really want to kiss her. But it's awkward. People are strolling by. This boy across the boardwalk is arguing with his dad that cotton candy won't spoil his dinner. And it's been sweltering all day. I don't want to know what I smell like.

"So . . . see you tomorrow," Skye says.

"Yeah. Tomorrow."

Then we go our separate ways.

five

Skye

the summer's out of reach

I CAN'T stop thinking about Seth.

The last time I saw him was two months ago. He hugged me on the boardwalk. He said he'd see me tomorrow.

But he never showed up.

I waited at that stupid seagull for an hour. Every time I see it, I'll be reminded of how expertly Seth played me.

Except it didn't feel like he was playing me. It felt real.

An orange leaf falls on our table in the courtyard. The breeze scrapes the leaf along the worn wooden surface, then wedges it against Jocelyn's water bottle. The leaf is offensive. It's orange. It fell off a tree. And this breeze isn't like the soft breeze at the beach when Seth kissed me. This breeze is chilly. It's all a harsh reminder that summer ended a long time ago.

I pull the sleeves of my sweater over my hands.

"Maybe I'll wrap myself in a big red bow and let him do dirty things to me," Kara says.

"Like he doesn't do dirty things to you already," Jocelyn snickers.

"Well, these can be new things. Boys need sexual adventure or they get bored."

"I highly doubt Dillon is bored," I say.

"I totally caught him checking out that girl at the mall, remember?"

"The porn-star wannabe?"

"No, the one who looked like Lani."

"Do you seriously think anyone could compete with you?"

Kara is gorgeous. Boys take one look at her emerald eyes and long, black hair and are reduced to slobbering idiots. It happens everywhere we go. She's part Colombian, so she has this whole exotic thing going on. Kara has been known to flirt with supercute boys, but just for fun. She's been with Dillon for almost two years. Their anniversary is coming up. Kara wants to surprise him with something special.

"Dillon's crazy about you," I say.

"And I'd be crazy not to keep it that way," Kara says.

"What about that idea you had last night?" I ask. "Getting backstage passes for Residue?"

"You guys talked last night?" Jocelyn interjects. "I was waiting for you to call me back."

"Sorry," I tell her. "I fell asleep on my English essay."

Jocelyn picks up her cookie. She immediately puts it back down.

"You should go talk to Luke," Kara tells Jocelyn. Jocelyn has been crushing on Luke since last year. But she's too shy to talk to him. We're all about following your heart, so she must really be afraid of rejection. I agree with Kara that Jocelyn should face her fear. She looks adorable today in her floaty Anthropologie dress and floral blazer. I'm sure Luke would think she's sweet.

"I'm not going back in until we have to," Jocelyn says.

"Luke's not in the caf. He's right over there."

"Oh my god he's *out* here?" Jocelyn ducks down as if expecting an air raid. "Why is he out here? He's never out here."

"Guess he heard you were out here," Kara says. "Ooh." She takes out her mini cam to film something for A Day in the Life, her website that has a huge following. Half the time I never know what she's filming until I see her new videos. A Day in the Life isn't about any one thing. It's kind of about everything. In the past few weeks, Kara has done videos on:

* the world's largest paper clip collection
* academic inequality in areas of the world where girls aren't allowed to attend school
* why no two snowflakes are exactly alike
* our lacking health care system
* the search for the ultimate cheesecake
* the prevalence of impostor tomatoes that look perfect but taste horrible
* teens who knit

Whatever Kara thinks is interesting enough to show, she shows it. Her videos have deeper messages. Like the one featuring little dogs from around town. You could watch it purely for the smiles. Or you could reflect on the bond we share with our pets and how they're like family members. It was all in the way

Kara blended the music with clips of people hugging their dogs at the end.

"You're *filming* him?" Jocelyn is incredulous.

"Of course not. I'm filming Connor's candy bar. My next video's on old-school candy. Remember Sky Bars from when we were little? Whatever happened to them?"

"Is he looking?" Jocelyn asks me.

"Just go over and say hey," Kara tells her. "Pretend you're getting a drink or something. His table is on the way."

"The last thing I need is more cookie temptation."

Jocelyn is amazing. She's the sweetest person I know. She rocks killer looks every single day, organizes donations for homeless shelters in New York City, and volunteers for One World with me. That's our school's environmental club. But Jocelyn has a weird obsession with celebrity diets. For some reason, she thinks she's fat. Which is ridiculous.

"How do you expect something to happen with Luke if you're not even on his radar?" Kara asks.

"I was hoping he'd notice me without having to make a spectacle of myself."

"Going up to him for two seconds is not making a spectacle. It's what people do."

Jocelyn picks up her cookie again. "Why did I buy this?" She puts the cookie down on its mini plastic tray, shoves it across the table, and says, "Get this thing away from me."

Kara breaks off a piece of the cookie. "Chocolate peanut-butter chip?"

Jocelyn nods.

"I love these."

Jocelyn watches Kara chew.

"Um, I know we've gone over this like a million times," I say, "but can we revisit the Seth thing again?"

"You weren't the only one who felt it," Jocelyn reiterates. "Seth was totally into you."

"Then why didn't he show up the next day?"

"Anything could have happened. If there was a way for him to be there, he would have been there."

"What was the point of it all? Why string someone along like that just to have it go nowhere?"

"He wasn't stringing you along."

"Why are boys *like* this?"

"Because they can be," Kara explains. "They can be manipulative asses and play as many mind games as they want and there will always be some girl desperate enough to fall for it. Boys are, like, rewarded for being scumbags."

"But I know we connected," I insist. "We had *so* much fun, you guys. Why would he kiss me if he didn't like me?"

"If he felt the same way, he would have been there," Kara says. The first time she said this was when I called her that day Seth didn't show. It was really harsh to hear. But now I'm starting to believe that Kara is right. Only . . . Seth felt like a soul mate. How could I have been the only one to feel it?

"He totally liked you," Jocelyn says. "I'm telling you, something happened and he couldn't meet up. There could be a million reasons why."

Kara shakes her head. "When you're trying to figure out why some boy acted like a dumbass? The most obvious answer is usually the right one."

"Which is?" Jocelyn asks. She throws the half of her lunch she didn't eat back into her lunch bag.

"He was just having fun," Kara says. "Girls always read way more into these things. Just because it felt all intense to her doesn't mean it was for him."

"Don't hold back," I say. "Tell us how you really feel."

Kara's face softens. "Sorry, Skye. I know you really liked Seth. I just hate to see you obsess over him when there are so many boys here dying to go out with you."

Been there. Over that. I've gone out with some of these boys. Those relationships didn't last long enough to mean much. The kind of connection I so desperately wanted never happened. It was like I was forcing myself to act happy instead of actually being happy. I was starting to think I was being an impossible romantic. That maybe what I wanted didn't exist in real life. But after this summer, I know it does. How it felt to be with Seth was undeniable. After experiencing how amazing that immediate attraction was, there's no going back to mediocrity. Why should I have to settle for someone who doesn't understand me the way Seth did?

"Hey, Skye," Ben says, passing our table. He sits next to me in English. I'm getting to know him better since he's been talking to me a lot more this year. We were only acquaintances before.

"Hey," I say back.

"Did you finish that essay?"

"Yeah, at like three in the morning."

"I didn't even go to sleep."

"Impressive."

"You too. Way to show the last minute who's boss."

I smile halfheartedly. Ben tries to be funny. He doesn't quite pull it off.

Kara is probably right. It's only something real if both people feel it. Even so, I have my half of our photo-booth picture strip taped up in my locker. Just in case.

six

Seth

you can't always get what you want

IT WOULD probably be a lot easier to work on this huge collage in one of the art studios. Those studios are sick. All that space and natural light. But you have to take an art class to use studio space. Which my business major doesn't allow. Fall semester of freshman year is notoriously jammed with general requirements.

Good thing I lucked out getting this suite instead of a double. Our room is big enough for me to set up an easel on my side. Which Grant doesn't hesitate to crash into on a consistent basis. It's much easier to work with big pieces of wood I snag from construction site Dumpsters or reclaimed plastic parts this way.

Reggatta de Blanc is playing for inspiration. Before Sting went solo, he was the lead singer of The Police. Before that, he was Gordon Sumner, history teacher. Sting's passion for history is why so many of his songs have a political message. I want to make art that means something, too.

I step back from the canvas to evaluate my progress.

This is crap. What am I even doing? Hanging pieces of glass tied with twine all over a statement about post-college life in these harsh economic times seemed like a good metaphor. But now it just looks busted. If I was trying to make a statement, the only statement I've made is "I am a failure."

The inspiration is gone.

Grant comes banging in. He face-plants on his bed.

"Is he here?" Grant muffles.

"Negative."

He sticks up a power fist.

A bathroom connects our room to the other room of our suite. Tim and Dorian are in the other room. Tim is cool. But Dorian needs to get a life. He's a hardcore gamer. Dorian is so hardcore that he's failing his classes because he can't stop gaming. He stays up until three or four in the morning, sometimes later. Grant's bed is up against the wall that has Dorian's TV on the other side. A very thin wall. A wall so thin it sounded like Modern Warfare was breaking out in our room every night for the first two weeks of class. Grant swears he's been shaken awake by vibrations from the game's explosions. We told Dorian to turn it down.

Dorian kept saying he would.

Modern Warfare kept breaking out in our room.

Grant and I had no choice. We reported Dorian to the RA. Now he has to use a headset. Oh, and he hates us. Dorian enjoys demonstrating his hatred by "forgetting" to use his headset sometimes. Like last night. Grant and I were up until five.

"We need to talk to him again," I say.

Grant turns over on his side, kicking his sneakers off. "You talk. I'll sleep."

"How does Tim ever sleep?"

"He's never there."

The man has a point. Tim was sexiled from his room our third night here. We were scandalized by the fact that Dorian managed to score with a girl so quickly. Tim spends a lot of time over here. But being sexiled gave him courage to talk to girls. If Dorian could do it, Tim knew he definitely could. Now he's friends with a few girls who let him sleep in their rooms. I guess they feel sorry for him.

Music starts blasting from the guys across the hall.

"Seriously?" Grant asks the door. He mashes the pillow over his head. "Freaks."

College is awesome in so many ways. The freedom. The new people. Getting to know yourself in a way that's impossible in high school. It's even better if you go to college in an interesting place. Penn is the best of both worlds—I'm getting an excellent education in an amazing city. It's just a short walk over the bridge to Center City, the coolest part of Philly. I'll bring my sketchbook and hang out at Rittenhouse Square or a coffeehouse. Or I'll explore. I've gotten tons of new artwork ideas just from walking around. Inspiration is everywhere. The energy feeds my soul.

But one way college sucks is that you're forced to live with people you don't know. Grant is kind of pretentious. His personality can be summed up by this Kierkegaard quote on the poster taped over his bed: "PEOPLE UNDERSTAND ME SO POORLY THAT THEY DON'T EVEN UNDERSTAND MY COMPLAINT ABOUT THEM NOT UNDERSTANDING ME." Grant is a philosophy major. He is always philosophizing. His personal philosophy apparently includes a reverence of entropy, because his side of the room is disgusting. I'm not saying I wash my sheets often enough. But I don't think Grant has washed his sheets *ever*. There are used bowls with mold growing in them on his desk. Dirty clothes are heaped all around. He never helps clean the bathroom. Ironically, Grant's lack of interest in decreasing his gross-out factor does not prevent him from believing he's better than everyone else.

The guys across the hall turn their music up.

"I have to get out of here," Grant says. He sits up and puts his shoes back on. "Want to grab dinner?"

"Yeah." Grant might not be my favorite person, but other than Tim he's pretty much the only friend I have here. And I need real food. This girl Karen from my economics class gave me some cookies she made today. The tin is already half empty.

We grab the elevator. Just as the doors are closing, someone yells, "Hold it!" A hand reaches in to force the doors open. Two guys from our floor get on. "Hey, Grant," one of them says.

"Hey."

"How's that philosophy major working out for you?"

"Probably better than ignorance is working out for you."

"Oooh, *burn!*" taunts the guy's friend. "You just got

schooled."

"Let's see who gets schooled ten years from now when I'm a CEO and this loser's washing my car." The guys pound fists.

Grant doesn't have a comeback. He doesn't feel the need to have one. He's entirely confident about being a philosophy major.

As we cross High Rise Field, Grant asks me why I'm not an art major. He's recently taken an interest in my collages.

"It's not realistic," I say.

"How so?"

"You can't make a living as an artist."

"What do you think all the artists making a living as artists are doing?"

"Representing an extremely small percentage of the population."

"Ah, so you admit it *is* realistic," Grant counters in his irritating philosophy-snob tone.

"No, it's not. What are you going to do with a philosophy major?"

"Irrelevant. I'm living in the Now. The Now is all we ever have."

"Well, some of us have to make a living in the Later."

"Doesn't it bother you that the only reason you're a business major is for the money?"

"Of course it does. I hate it. If I start acting like the douches in my classes, you have permission to kill me."

"Then why are you torturing yourself?"

"Because I don't have a choice!" I snap. In an ideal world, I'd be studying what I care about. That's what would make me happy. But not everyone gets to be happy. Some of us have to put other people first. Like my mom. She used to be an administrative assistant for a construction contractor. Then she started having serious health problems. None of the doctors could figure out what was wrong with her. She was exhausted all the time, her stomach hurt, and she kept throwing up. One doctor who actually took the time to talk with her for more than three seconds referred her to an excellent specialist. They never figured out exactly what was wrong. She took too many sick days and lost her job. Now she's feeling a little better, but she hasn't been able to find a new job. Who's going to take care of her when she's old with Dad out of the picture?

Grant can piss away his entire college education. He doesn't have to worry about the future. His parents are loaded. Most of the kids at Penn come from rich families. They probably all have summer houses like those insane ones in Sea Bright.

Sea Bright. The last time I was truly happy.

I can't believe how epically I fucked that up.

My mom came to pick me up super early the morning I was supposed to meet up with Skye. Mom didn't even tell me her doctor's appointment got switched. I begged her to let me stay. I promised that Dad would drive me home. But she couldn't wait to get us out of there. I left a note at the seagull statue where I was supposed to meet Skye. There wasn't anywhere to wedge it. I would have given anything for a freaking piece of tape. All I could do was prop the note up against the bottom of the seagull. It had all my contact info.

I guess Skye never found it.

Stupid. I was so stupid not to get her info the night we met. But it never even occurred to me as a remote possibility that I wouldn't see her the next day. We don't even know each others' last names. There's no way to search for her online.

I asked Nick if he knew Skye. He didn't. Not that it matters. I couldn't go there anyway.

I loved Chloe. Chloe loved me. If a girl I loved who loved me back could just walk away like what we had was nothing, if my dad could abandon my mom after everything they'd been through, couldn't anyone?

Then what's the point?

seven

Skye

dreams, they complicate my life

THE BEST dreams are those really intense romantic ones where the dream still lingers for hours after you wake up. If you are very lucky, the dream lingers for days. I had one of those dreams last night.

About Seth.

I remember how it felt to be with him so clearly. As if it was just yesterday instead of six months ago.

I've been wondering what it will be like going back to Sea Bright this summer. What it will be like to see Seth again. But I don't even know if he'll be there. And summer is forever away.

"You're dripping," Jocelyn notifies me.

Earth to Skye: pay attention. You're at a One World meeting. We're all painting banners for our new green living initiative. The "green" part of "go green" should be painted green. Not green with blue blobs.

"Unless you're going for an Earth effect," Jocelyn says.

"No. I was . . . thinking about last summer."

"Another Seth dream?"

"Oh yeah." This isn't the first time I've had a lingering dream about Seth. They've been happening more frequently for some reason.

As I'm blotting up the blue blobs, Kara comes over to where Jocelyn and I are painting our banner on the floor.

"Can we leave at four thirty instead of four?" she asks. "I want to film drama, but they don't start rehearsing until four. I'm doing a segment on their adaptation of *Grease*."

"That's cool," I say. "It'll give me more time to wreck another banner."

"Hey, congrats on hitting a hundred thousand!" Jocelyn tells Kara. "That's awesome."

"Thanks," Kara says flatly.

Getting 100,000 subscribers for A Day in the Life had been Kara's goal for a really long time. She was obsessed, actually. It was like hitting that number was going to make her feel way more important on top of already having tons of adoring fans. But as soon as she hit it, she immediately started talking about hitting 150. It doesn't seem like she's even appreciating this achievement she worked so hard for. Or maybe she's just in a bad mood about Dillon.

"See you guys out front." As Kara leaves, she says bye to Lani, the president of One World.

"Is there anyone Kara *doesn't* know?" Jocelyn asks.

"Not really. The girl's a superstar."

"So like . . . did she say anything to you about Dillon?"

"Only what we already know."

"I wonder why she was fronting for so long that everything

was fine." Jocelyn reaches for the purple paint. "We're her best friends. Why would she pretend with us?"

"It's embarrassing to admit your relationship isn't what you want it to be." I should know. Every boy I've been with has been a colossal disappointment. Except Seth.

"But if you can't tell your best friends, who can you tell?"

"She didn't want to tell anyone. I guess she was hoping things would get better."

We don't talk for a while. We just paint. I always feel kind of awkward when Jocelyn and I talk about Kara. Or when Kara and I talk about Jocelyn. Not that it stops me.

"I wonder if sex has to be like that," Jocelyn says.

"Like what?"

"Like once you do it, you can't ever go back to just kissing."

Kara and Dillon got in a huge fight the other night. They were making out in her room. That's all Kara wanted to do. She didn't feel like having sex. She told me that ever since they starting having sex last year, Dillon expects every time they make out to end in sex. When Kara told Dillon that she didn't feel like it, he took offense. He accused her of not wanting him anymore. But of course that wasn't true. She just didn't want him *right then*.

Dillon stormed out. They're still not talking.

"It's a problem without a solution," I say.

"Exactly. She doesn't want to break up, but they can't go back to how they were before."

"She said she wants the magic back. She wants things to feel like they did when they started going out."

"How is sex only exciting for the first year? That doesn't seem right."

"I don't think it's like that for everyone. Maybe . . ."

"What?"

"I don't know. Maybe they're not the best match."

"But they always look happy. Oh, crap." Jocelyn puts her brush down. She holds out her metallic silver scarf and wipes off some purple paint that dripped on it. "Anyway. This is the first big fight they've had."

"That we know of. You can never know everything that goes on in someone else's relationship. Not even the people in the relationship know everything."

"Does Ben know about Seth?"

"No." Ben and I have been going out for two months. He calls me his girlfriend and everything. He's a great guy. But I don't think of him as my boyfriend. I've never even called him that.

Lani puts her banner on the table to dry. She drew different examples of how to reduce our environmental footprint. There are sections for things like planting trees, carpooling, and reusing. Lani's so passionate about protecting our planet. She's definitely going into environmental science. It must be awesome to know what you want to do. I know that I want to make the world a better place. I just don't know exactly how yet.

Jocelyn and I squeeze into our puffy coats and hats and gloves and scarves. While we're waiting outside for Kara, it starts snowing. Jocelyn and I have a lot of things in common. Love of snow is not one of them. What can I say? I'm a devoted summer girl.

"Woo!" Jocelyn runs around in circles. She loves everything about snow. Playing in it, making snowmen with it, sledding on it. Snow reverts Jocelyn right back to kindergarten. But this relentless frosty February makes me want summer to get here even faster.

I stand under the snow looking up at the big, white sky. I wish I knew where Seth was right now. He could be anywhere. He's probably at some college far away. But what if he's not that far? Is it snowing where he is? It kills me to think that he could be somewhere close to New Jersey—or maybe even *in* New Jersey—but there's no way for me to find out.

"Sorry, sorry!" Kara comes over to us. "When did it start snowing?"

"A few minutes ago," I say.

"And Jocelyn hasn't made a snowman yet?"

"It's not going to stick," Jocelyn intuits.

"How do you know?" I ask.

"Look how slushy it is on the ground."

"All I can think about is hot chocolate," Kara says. "Let's go."

This isn't just any hot chocolate. We're talking decadent hot chocolate made with three different kinds of chocolate. It's legendary. The best part is that it comes with a fluffy rectangle of homemade marshmallow deliciousness melted right on top.

When we get to The Fountain, we're stoked that our couch is free. The Fountain is this old-school ice-cream parlor with stools along the counter and cute tables scattered all over. But we aren't interested in sitting anywhere except the purple velvet couch.

Jocelyn runs over to our couch. She throws her bag down to claim it. Then she spins around and gestures with flair. "VIP seating, ladies?"

There's nothing like being all toasty warm inside with your best friends when it's freezing out. We get our hot chocolates and scrunch up on the couch with Kara in the middle.

"Where's your marshmallow?" Kara asks Jocelyn.

"New diet," Jocelyn explains. "No white foods."

It breaks my heart whenever Jocelyn goes on a new diet. She's beautiful just the way she is. But she never listens when I tell her that. It's like there's something driving her to keep searching for the perfect diet that will make her flawless.

"So how'd it go at drama?" I ask Kara.

"Okay. I'm not sure yet. Aiden Harris was distracting me."

"With his gorgeousness?"

"What else?"

"His *eyes*," Jocelyn swoons.

"His *everything*," I add.

"But I think I can cobble together a decent clip," Kara says.

"Um, I'm pretty sure Miss Hundred Thousand will come up with something brilliant," I say.

"Whatever. The kittens girl has over a million subscribers."

"The kittens girl is intellectually challenged," I remind her. "Are you really comparing A Day in the Life to those other channels? Even the good ones aren't as successful. That Art Thoughtz guy has way less subscribers than you and he's freaking hilarious."

"Beyond hilarious," Jocelyn says. "Did you see that one

where he's labeling everyday objects as art and he shows this dude sleeping on the couch and he's like, 'Your unemployed brother in his forties who doesn't do anything and lives with your mom? Art!'"

"And it's performance art, so—"

"Double art!" we yell.

An older couple sharing a sundae darts us annoyed looks. It's hard to calm down when we get like this. I love it when the three of us are on a friends high. Our voices go up about ten notches in volume. We get all giddy and squealy and everything cracks us up. I can tell the friends high is making Kara feel better. Her bad mood is rapidly disintegrating.

"I like those paranoid vegetables," I continue.

"I like the guy who *plays* the vegetables," Jocelyn says.

"A Day in the Life needs something with vegetables," Kara decides.

"Singing vegetables," I suggest.

"Vegetables on *fire*!" Jocelyn exclaims.

Sundae couple is alarmed.

"No, then she'd be like that dude who blows stuff up all day," I say.

"How many subscribers does he have?" Kara wants to know.

"You are not going to blow stuff up to get subscribers. Look how many you already have just by being you. Keep it classy."

"Like the guy who blows his nose and then shows everyone?" Jocelyn asks.

"Eeeeewww!" Kara and I shriek.

Sundae couple is not happy.

"Keep it down, children, you're scaring the grownups," Kara warns.

"That guy who rants about the end of the world is scary," Jocelyn says.

"Scary insane," Kara clarifies. "Paranoid rants are *so* last year."

"You don't need to be gimmicky," I assure Kara. "Everyone loves you."

"They'll love me even more for sharing the magnificence that is Aiden Harris. Assuming I concentrated long enough to turn my camera on. How could I let him distract me so easily?"

"Aiden Harris distracts everybody," Jocelyn says. "It's the law."

"Dillon would kill me if he knew we were flirting."

"Not if Aiden was doing all the flirting," I say.

Kara gazes up at the ceiling, sipping her hot chocolate. The exaggerated innocent act isn't fooling anyone.

"How much flirting are we talking about?"

"Enough for him to know I'm interested."

Jocelyn and I exchange a look behind Kara.

"I didn't know you were that mad at Dillon," Jocelyn says.

"Of course I'm mad! How would you feel if your boyfriend expected sex every time he came over?"

"I wouldn't know," Jocelyn mumbles.

"We used to be happy. I wanted to do it all the time. But now it's just like . . . everything is about sex. If I don't feel like doing it, Dillon takes it personally. If I do feel like it, he's worried that I'm not really into it. Why is he making it so complicated?"

"Sex complicates things," Jocelyn says.

"This from someone who's never even had a boyfriend," Kara fires back. She's gripping her mug so tightly I'm surprised it doesn't crack into a million pieces.

Jocelyn blinks at her.

"I'm sorry," Kara says. "I'm in a vile mood. I should go."

"No!" I grab Kara's arm. "Don't go."

"It's okay. I have a ton of work to do if I want to overhaul the site by next month." Kara gets up and puts on her coat. "Later."

We watch Kara leave. Unexpectedly coming down from a friends high is a hard crash.

"You guys didn't even notice those boys, did you?" Jocelyn asks.

"What boys?"

"I knew it."

"What boys?"

"Over there." Jocelyn tilts her head in their direction.

I look over. Two cute boys are sitting by the window. I might recognize them from school, but I'm not sure.

"They're cute and all, but . . ."

"But you already have a boyfriend."

"Is that what we're calling him now?"

"And Kara already has a boyfriend," Jocelyn sighs. She sips her hot chocolate without marshmallows. I wish she wasn't depriving herself of their fluffy deliciousness.

"What's going on with you?" I ask.

"Boys always notice you and Kara. They never notice me. Don't get me wrong—I'm happy for you guys. Or I try to be. It's like my self-esteem tank gets stuck on empty sometimes."

"Aw." I slide over to Jocelyn and put my arm around her. "Boys notice you."

"Not like they notice you."

"How long have you been feeling like this?"

"A long time."

"Why didn't you say anything?"

"Because I knew it would sound like I'm throwing a pity party. Aaaand it sounds like I'm throwing a pity party."

"No, it doesn't."

"We can't even have cake at this party. No white foods."

I squeeze her shoulder in sympathy.

"It just feels like I'll be alone forever."

"What about Luke?"

"What *about* Luke? He doesn't even know I exist."

"He would if you started talking to him."

"You mean where I start talking to him and I ask him out and he dies of laughter right in front of me? Thanks, I'll pass."

"You have to take a risk if you want things to change."

"You didn't have to. Ben started talking to you. Ben asked you out. Same with Kara and Dillon."

"But it's scary every time you get closer to someone," I say. "No matter who started it."

"Yeah, but it's less scary when you're not the one taking a risk."

"What happened to following your heart? Isn't that our thing?"

Jocelyn gulps the rest of her hot chocolate without marshmallows. The hopeless look in her eyes makes me sad. We've all been there. Feeling like things will never get better. Like we'll never find someone to love. But Jocelyn is amazing. She should totally take a chance on Luke. Following your heart means allowing the possibility of finding true love to be stronger than the fear of rejection.

The comforting smell of fresh pasta sauce greets me when I get home.

"Come help me chop the salad," Mom calls from the kitchen.

I love chopping salad. Salad tastes so much better when you chop it. Chopping all the vegetables into tiny pieces puts me in a cathartic zone.

"How was your day?" Mom asks.

"Okay." I take the romaine lettuce out of the strainer and pile it on a big wooden board. Then I slam the chopper down in the middle of the pile and start rocking it back and forth.

"Are you sure about that?" Mom says, watching me frantically chopping.

"Is anyone ever happy? Like, is happiness something you can actually achieve? Or is it just this elusive promise we keep chasing forever?"

"What brought this on?"

"I don't know. Everything."

Mom puts some peeled carrots on the chopping board. "Of course it's possible to be happy. But no one's happy every minute of every day. There are too many changing variables."

I think about Ben. He's such a good guy. Am I not happy with him because of something lacking between us? Or is it because of how happy I get whenever I think about being with Seth?

"I'm going to the movies with Ben Saturday night," I say.

"Be home by one."

My parents have always been cool about letting me do whatever. They give me a lot more freedom than other kids get. I like that I've earned their trust. Dad says it's because I've never given them any reason to doubt my judgment. They see me as a good girl who would never do anything shocking.

Cleaning out my desk drawers after dinner, I find the sparkly confetti I saved from last summer at the roller rink with Seth. First the dream. Then what I was saying to Jocelyn about following your heart. Now this.

I have to find him. There has to be a way.

eight

Seth

something's missing

"GIVE IT," Karen says.

"I don't think so."

"Give me my pen back!"

"*Shhhh!*" a girl at the next table hisses.

"Sorry," I say. The girl has a point. This is a library.

Karen crawls over to me on the couch we've been hogging for the past two hours. "Give," she whispers, "me . . . my . . . pen . . . back."

"I . . . don't . . . think . . . so."

"You're going down, Seth."

Various X-rated images featuring Karen flash through my mind.

This isn't the first time I've pictured her that way.

When I realized she was flirting with me in economics, I wasn't sure what to think. I noticed little things at first. Like how we always ran into each other in the dining hall at lunch. Or how she stopped by my room to say hi a few times when she doesn't even live in my dorm. Or how she made me those cookies for no reason.

Karen is warm and pretty and fun to hang out with. She understands where I'm coming from. I've heard that like minds find each other at college. She's practically the only person I've met here who doesn't have a trust fund. We're both on financial aid. Karen even has work-study. I would have been eligible for work-study if my dad's income wasn't thirty-eight dollars over the cutoff point.

When I'm with Karen, I can relax. She doesn't make me feel uptight like the rest of these Penn girls do. She made me believe that I might be ready to let someone in again. So we started going out.

But what we have lacks the magic of what I had with Skye. When you have a strong connection with someone instantly, when it feels like you've known them forever even though you've just met, the intensity is undeniable. That's how it was with Skye. Undeniable. Karen obviously wants things to get serious with us. She's been so sweet that I hate letting her down. If I couldn't go there with Skye, there's no way letting Karen in would measure up.

Karen crawls on my lap. She reaches for the pen I'm holding up. "Do you really want to get in trouble?" she purrs. "Wharton frowns on library escapades."

I give Karen her pen back. Then I get up to stretch. Passing by a window, I notice that it's snowing. A girl at the table by the window reminds me of Skye. They don't really look alike. It's just something about the way she is, the way she's tilting her head as she reads, how she's sitting with one foot up on her chair.

And I'm right back there again. Right back on the beach last summer. Kissing Skye.

I have to find her. There has to be a way.

Later when I'm alone in my room, I start working on a mix for Skye. I know it sounds crazy, but it seems like making this mix will increase the probability of finding her. This sudden need to find her hit me so hard it apparently knocked the logic part of my brain out.

My dad calls while I'm working on the mix.

"How's school going?" he asks.

"Same old. This douche in my management class had a nervous breakdown today. That was entertaining."

"Sounds like good times."

"Don't underestimate the pressure of being a business major."

Silence from Dad's end.

"You still there?" I check.

"You don't sound happy."

"Are *you*?"

"Honestly? I've been better."

Dad sounds run down. He might be regretting his decision to leave Mom. Maybe he's finally realizing that he can't be happy without her.

"Things aren't turning out the way I expected," he admits.

There it is. He knows he made a mistake. He wants to get back together with Mom.

Someone knocks on my door.

"It's open!" I yell.

Karen comes in. It's obviously freezing out. Her nose is red and she has two scarves wrapped around her neck.

"Who's that?" Dad asks.

"Karen's here."

"I'll let you go then."

"No, it's okay."

"Never keep a pretty girl waiting, Seth. Tell Karen I said hi."

"Will do." I hang up. "My dad says hi."

"How's he doing?"

"Realizing the error of his ways."

"What do you mean?"

"I think he wants to get back together with my mom."

Karen squeals. She throws her arms around me, jumping up and down. "That's awesome! Did he tell your mom yet?"

"I don't think so." I hope he talks to Mom about it soon. She's been miserable since Dad left. I've been worried about her. She'll be psyched to hear that he regrets leaving. I totally understand wanting your freedom. But not when you're a middle-aged married guy. Not when you've already found your person. Mom is Dad's person. From the stories they've told about all their years together, it's clear she always has been.

"We have to celebrate," Karen says.

It's cool when Karen gets excited about my life. She makes me feel like when good things happen to me, they're happening to her, too. Which is comforting to a neurotic freak like me. Being with Karen also balances things out with Grant. As hard as it is to believe, Grant has a girlfriend. Her name is Astor. Astor isn't revolting at all. She's actually really nice. What she sees in Grant is beyond me.

The four of us are going to Diner on the Square for dinner. Karen, Astor, and I are all packed into our winter gear for the walk down to Center City. Grant has on the same jacket he's worn since the fall. He's not even wearing a hat.

"Aren't you cold?" Karen asks him.

"I refuse to subscribe to cold," Grant declares.

"What does that even mean?" I ask.

"Cold is a state of mind. If you give in to cold, it will win. But if you accept that you have control over your perception of cold, you can alter your state of being."

"Isn't cold, like, a temperature?" Astor says.

"Only because we classify it as such."

"Um, fifteen degrees is cold whether or not we want to believe it. Are you seriously trying to tell us that you're warm?"

"Not warm. Just not giving in to cold."

"Then why are your ears red?"

Grant scoffs. "We don't have control over all of our physical responses to external stimuli. We can only control our internal reactions."

"I'm pretty sure I'd still think it's cold if I wasn't wearing my hat and coat and everything."

"Why don't you take them off and see?"

"No way! It's freezing!"

"Only because you're allowing yourself to be influenced by your environment."

"You mean the environment that's freezing?"

"Maybe you'd see my point if you were more open-minded."

"Maybe you'd admit you're cold if you were less obnoxious!"

Karen and I hang back as the latest Grant versus Astor Debate rages on.

"Why is he like this?" Karen mutters.

"Wish I knew."

Grant wasn't this bad when they first started going out. He was probably relieved to find a girl he could tolerate in our rotting society. But the past few weeks have been crazy. Grant has to attack everything Astor says. He feels the need to correct her in the most insulting ways. Astor shouldn't be treated like this. No one should. Hanging out with them has become painfully awkward.

The wind slices my face as we cross the bridge. When we get to the stairs that go down from the bridge to one of the residential streets, I point them out to Karen. That's the area I want to live in when I get my own place junior year. Preferably on Pine Street in the Twenties near that old-school soda fountain. It's such a mellow street, but it's only a few blocks from the action of Rittenhouse Square.

We follow Grant and Astor into Diner on the Square. Astor glares at Grant as we slide into a booth.

"Who's feeling breakfast for dinner?" Karen says.

"Definitely," I say.

Grant puts his menu down. He squints at Astor. "How can you believe there's some idyllic afterlife above the clouds?"

"Can you stop disrespecting my religion?" Astor fires back. "That's what I learned growing up."

"Did you not learn about atmospheric layers?"

I have no idea how their argument morphed from defining cold into what happens after you die. Too bad their argument didn't die before we got here.

Karen and I hide behind our big menus. Her wide eyes are like, *Seriously with this?*

"The notion of an afterlife is preposterous," Grant argues.

"Our souls are energy," Astor says. "That energy has to go somewhere."

"Yet you don't believe in reincarnation."

"Because I believe in heaven and hell."

"And where's hell, exactly? In the asthenosphere? The outer core?"

I shoot a warning look at Grant to shut up. He remains oblivious.

"I'm thinking pancakes," Karen announces.

"Blueberry?" I inquire.

"Of course."

Astor turns to Grant. "If you're so sure there's no after-life, why isn't it a known fact?"

"Most people aren't smart enough to deal with the truth. Believing in an afterlife is their response to fear. Their anti-quated beliefs give them something to cling to."

"Are you saying I'm stupid for not agreeing with you?"

"Let's just say that people who blindly follow organized religion aren't known for being particularly intelligent."

"Dude," I say. "No one knows what happens after you die. It's all a matter of opinion."

"Ah, but there *is* such a thing as a stupid opinion," Grant says.

"Yeah . . . I'm done." Astor slides out of the booth and grabs her coat from the rack.

"I'm going with her," Karen tells me. "Call me later?"

"Okay."

And then it's just me and my douchey roommate. And blueberry pancakes.

nine

Skye

all the roads lead back to you

"OH MY god!" Adrienne gasps, grabbing my arm. "That's him!"

"Where?" I frantically search in the direction she's looking.

"Wait. Sorry, it's the guy from yesterday again."

Adrienne thought she saw Seth yesterday. These guys were playing volleyball while she was laying out. One of them looked a lot like Seth. Adrienne and Seth didn't meet last summer, but Adrienne kind of remembers what he looks like from the party. I was gardening with my mom when Adrienne called to report the Seth sighting we'd been waiting for all summer. Of course I went running down to the beach. But it wasn't him.

We've been looking for Seth everywhere.

Ben is history. Not that three months with a boy I wasn't in love with is much history. Seth is the only boy for me. My stomach has been churning all summer with anticipation that he might be coming back. What if he comes back and he hardly remembers me? Or he has a girlfriend? Every day I hope I'll see him. Every day I'm disappointed.

Adrienne is attempting to cheer me up at the snowball place.

"May I have a spearmint lemonade?" I order.

"What happened to watermelon tangerine?" Adrienne asks.

"It's time to mix things up."

"Sorry about the false alarms. He'll be here. We'll find him. I just know it."

Right when Adrienne is saying, "I just know it," "Heart of Glass" comes on.

"No. Way." I gape at the ceiling.

"What?"

"This song. It was totally playing at the roller rink with Seth last year."

"Sweet."

"You know who this is, right?"

"Um . . ."

"Blondie! How can you not know Blondie?"

"Might I remind you that *you* didn't even know Blondie before your iPod got Sethified?"

"The same song comes on? Right when we were talking about him? It's a sign."

"It's totally a sign," Adrienne confirms.

As we're leaving the snowball place, a guy blocks the door with his ginormous dragon kite. He's trying to come in while angling his kite to avoid wedging it in the door frame. He doesn't see us trying to get out. There's some kind of kite festival this weekend. Either that or a bunch of kite enthusiasts have taken over the beach.

Adrienne peers around the kite. "Uh, excuse me? Can we get out?"

"Oh!" Dragon Kite says. "Didn't see you there." He steps back so we can leave.

"Let's check over there." I point to the biggest bunch of people flying kites on the beach. We're checking everyone and everything.

Kites are cool. There's enormous butterfly ones and ones with lots of flapping ribbons and brightly colored spiral ones. I scan the crowd to see if Seth is flying one of these kites. I don't even know if he likes kites. How wrong is it that I don't even know if he likes kites? And that I might never get the chance to find out?

Adrienne checks the time. "I have to leave soon."

"Another secret rendezvous with Greg?"

"You know how we love sneaking around," she grumbles.

Adrienne's mother doesn't approve of Greg. He's a townie. Adrienne met him when she went to dinner with her parents at the Italian restaurant where Greg is a waiter. According to Adrienne, Greg took one look at her and knew they had to be together. According to Mrs. Nova, Adrienne could do much better. Adrienne will be grounded for the rest of the summer if Mrs. Nova catches them together again.

"Not that the sneaking around is worth it anymore," Adrienne says. "Greg's being weird."

"Like how?"

"Like he won't call me back. He used to always call me back right away when he missed my calls."

"Is he working more hours?"

"Not that I know of. But I don't really know anything. He's been ignoring me for three days now. Why is it that we wished for boy action for years, then when we finally get some it comes with all this drama? Can't we ever have one perfect summer with boys? Just one freaking *summer*?"

"Seriously." I take one last desperate look around for Seth. "Okay. I'm going to check one more place and then I'm going home. Try not to worry about Greg. He's probably just been busy."

"Right, because summer is such a busy time."

"It is for restaurants. Hello, tourist season! He might have picked up an extra shift."

"If by 'extra shift' you mean 'another girl,' then yeah."

"Just promise me you'll talk to him."

"Fine. But when I show up at your house later dying of a broken heart because Greg admitted that he's lusting after some other girl, it will be your job to fix me."

"Deal."

I head over to the roller rink. Of course I've already checked there a few times this summer. But you never know when things might turn around.

My eyes take a minute to adjust to the dimly lit rink after being out in the bright sunlight. It's empty. I've never seen it this desolate before. Right when I'm about to leave, a middle-aged guy in skinny black jeans, a Led Zeppelin concert tee, and a heavy silver chain with dog tags comes out from the back.

"Rolling solo?" he says.

"What fun would that be?"

"You'd be surprised. People tend to let their inhibitions down when no one else is looking."

"I love coming here with my friends. I have a lot of sweet memories of this place."

"Can't say I don't have some of those myself." He extends his hand for me to shake. "I'm Pete."

"I'm Skye."

"Nice to meet you, Skye. Can I offer you a Yoo-hoo?"

"Thanks! I love Yoo-hoo."

Pete goes behind the counter to the bar. I sit on one of the stools.

"Here you go," Pete says, expertly sliding the full glass over to me. "One sec." He roots around below the counter. Then he locates a box of crazy straws. He puts a hot-pink crazy straw in my glass. "The finishing touch. Enjoy."

"You even have crazy straws? Could this place be any better?"

"Not really. It'll be a sad day when it shuts down at the end of the season."

"What?"

"Business hasn't been good for a while now. Hard to believe this old place is losing money every day."

"But Wheel in the Sky can't close! I've been coming here since I was nine!"

"You should have seen it back in its heyday." Pete shakes his head slowly, remembering. "When we first opened, there was a line for skates. It was packed every night. The place had an electric vibe, you know? And now . . ."

We look around the empty rink.

"But it's early," I say. "People will come in later."

"I wouldn't count on it. Most nights don't get much more crowded than this."

"That's just wrong."

"Couldn't agree more. I've poured my soul into this place for twenty-two years. To watch it go under . . . well, that's something I never thought I'd see."

"It's so fun here. I love the whole eighties theme."

"There's a reason for that." Pete leans forward conspiratorially. "I met my wife in the eighties. She taught me how to skate. Truth is, I've been holding on to this place way past when I should have sold it. It reminds me of everything we were. When we were young."

"Oh, I'm sorry. Is she . . . did she—"

"We separated last year. That's when I moved here, to be closer to the rink. A few guys were running it for me before. But now . . ." Pete looks at me. "Rambling! Sorry for the novel."

"That's okay."

"You're a good listener. You remind me of my son. I can't bear to tell him the place is closing, though. He'd be crushed."

For what might be the last time, I take in the vintage Coke bottles, the retro posters covering the walls, the neon Rubik's Cube flashing over the doorway to the bathrooms. I can't imagine this place not existing anymore. It just doesn't seem possible.

"What's going to happen to all of this cool stuff?" I ask.

"Guess I'll take some of it home. Most of it will have to go."

"You can't find stuff like this anywhere. It's sad that so much

classic Americana is disappearing. It's like people don't appreciate meaningful connections anymore."

Pete gives me a wistful smile. "You are very wise, Skye."

"I just have one question."

"Shoot."

"If you've held on to the rink because it reminds you of your
wife, then why aren't you together?" As soon as the words leave
my mouth, I wish I could take them back. That's way too personal a question to ask someone I've known for three seconds.

Pete gives me a wistful smile again. "Have I mentioned how
wise you are?"

ten

Seth

make the sun shine from pure desire

THERE'S SOMETHING incredibly relaxing about kites. The smooth way they glide on air currents. How their shiny parts glimmer in the sunlight. You could come out here with your kite and bask in the sea breeze and forget about everything that's bothering you.

Or not.

I'm worried that I won't find Skye. My plan was to come back to Sea Bright in June and start looking for her. Then we'd have the whole summer together. It would have been epic. Except there was this summer session art class I was dying to take. I had to go for it. The next three years are going to be even more demanding than this year was. The thought of graduating without taking a single art class was way too depressing. Getting to use the sick studio space and learning new techniques was amazing. But finding Skye would be even more amazing.

I know she's here. I can feel it.

We'll find each other eventually. Unless she's still mad

at me for not showing up last year. What if she's already seen me? What if she's avoiding me? I have to tell her what really happened. Other than all the same places we went last year, I don't know where to look. One option is to stalk those McMansions on the hill until I find out which house is hers. But I'm pretty sure the neighbors would call the police on me for trespassing.

This kite festival makes me think about how different we all are. What makes one person obsess over stamp collecting while someone else has never even noticed stamps? Are our proclivities mostly due to environmental influences? Is a lifetime love of figurine collecting genetic? The awesome thing is that no matter how esoteric your interests are, you can probably find at least one other person who feels the same way. Or a whole bunch of people. Then excellence like this kite festival ensues.

These kites are crazy intricate. I was talking to some enthusiasts before who said that a lot of them were handmade by the owners. My favorite one is probably the big loop with all different shapes spiraling around. It's inspiring me to try a spiral collage. I found an old Slinky on the beach. Maybe I could stretch it out and work with it.

I'm craving shaved ice. So I go over to the snowball place and order a watermelon tangerine. Right after the cashier (snowbarista?) shouts my order to the woman pouring syrups, she calls out, "Black licorice is up!"

A guy hauling a gigantic dragon kite goes up to the counter to get his black licorice. As he's turning to leave, his kite bumps into a little girl. She drops her snowball. She takes a second to absorb that her snowball has been reduced to a pink ice splatter on the floor. Then she starts bawling.

"Sorry!" he says. "I really need to look where I'm going."

The evil dragon kite rustles triumphantly.

The girl's mom is trying to comfort her. She grabs a wad of napkins and mops up the spill.

I kneel down in front of the girl. "That was crazy, huh?"

She stops crying.

"Do you want a new snowball?"

She nods, wiping her cheek.

"That's nice of you," her mom says, "but we're fine."

"Please, I insist. What flavor was it?"

"Bubble gum. Thank you."

For what will probably be the only time, I order a bubble gum snowball. The girl stares at me. She's clearly still traumatized by a massive dragon kite swooping down on her. I grab my watermelon tangerine when it's called, waving to the girl on the way out. She smiles and waves back.

"Thanks again!" her mom calls after me.

This is one of the few gorgeous days August has delivered. August down the shore is pretty much synonymous with muggy. But today is cooler and less humid. There's even a perfect summer breeze. Just like that perfect summer breeze the night I kissed Skye.

I swing by my dad's house to pick up some cardboard, my glue stick, and a stack of paper strips I made from ripped magazine pages. I walk down the beach to our dune where we kissed. All the kite festival chaos is far enough away that I have this whole stretch of beach to myself. I climb to the top of our dune, remembering how Skye raced me up here. Remembering how beautiful she looked in the sunset. How she glowed as I pulled her close to me.

Three hours fly by. I've been trying to translate everything I feel for Skye into this collage. I want the art I make to be a physical representation of my emotions. When other people see my work, I want them to feel the exact same way I did when I was creating it.

I have to get back. Dad's grilling tonight. Some of his friends are coming over for dinner. Walking along the ocean's edge in the late afternoon light, I put my earbuds in and play "Waiting for a Girl Like You." Foreigner understood how I'm consumed with need.

The seagull statue taunts me on the boardwalk. How different would my life be if I'd met up with Skye when I was supposed to? Would we have tried a long-distance thing? Would it have worked?

Would she be thinking of sharing her life with me forever, the way I'm thinking about her?

I head back down the boardwalk toward Dad's house. This girl passes me and does a double take. I'd probably be too in my head to notice if she didn't look a lot like Skye. Same long, honey-blonde hair. Same Cali-girl look.

I glance at her over my shoulder.

She's staring at me.

"Hey," she says, running up to me. "Are you Seth?"

"Yeah."

"I saw you at that beach party last year."

"Oh, yeah. Sorry, I didn't recognize you."

"That's okay. We didn't meet. You were with my friend Skye."

My heart slams against my chest.

"Do you know where she is?" I ask.

"She should be at her house. I can take you there, if you want."

"Now?"

She nods.

"Cool," I say. I can't believe I was about to go home and shuck corn for the grill.

"I'm Adrienne, by the way."

"Seth. But you knew that."

"Totally! I mean, I thought it was you when I first saw you, but you were too far away to tell. And then when I got closer I was almost absolutely sure. But it wasn't until I passed you that I knew. I can't believe I found you! This is—" Adrienne stops abruptly. As if she's said too much.

Which means there's too much to say.

"Has Skye been . . . looking for me?" I ask.

"Sort of," Adrienne says in a calmer tone.

"So she's not mad?"

"Why would she be mad?"

"That I didn't show up last year?"

"No. Well, maybe at first. But not anymore."

"Good. Because I've been looking for her everywhere."

"Oh my god you *have*?" Excited Adrienne is back. "No way! How long have you been here? We've been looking for you everywhere, too! Where have you been?"

As I try to keep up with answering her questions, I become increasingly nervous. I can't believe I'm finally going to see Skye again. I can't believe she's been looking for me this whole time. I can't believe I'm wearing my ratty cargos and flip-flops with this ripped R.E.M. shirt. At least I have a new batch of friendship bracelets from Jade. Skye loves those.

We get to the parking lot. Adrienne says, "This is me." Not surprised that "me" is a shiny, red Beemer. I'd normally scoff that Adrienne is driving us up the hill instead of walking. But it would take like half an hour to walk. I can't stand the waiting anymore.

"This. Is *awesome*," Adrienne gushes.

Awesome doesn't even begin to describe it. Good thing I broke up with Karen in April. She kept pressuring me to get serious. She wanted this big commitment. She even wanted me to spend spring break with her family. Basically, Karen wanted way more than I was ready to give.

We pull up to a gorgeous modern beach house. I'm down with the boxy design. Lots of glass walls. Airy interiors. It must be amazing inside.

Adrienne turns off the car.

No one moves.

"Ready?" she asks.

"Definitely. There was just so much buildup—"

"I know!" she shrieks with a burst of nervous giggling. I guess nervous is contagious.

We get out. We walk across the fancy tiled entryway. Then we're at the door.

Skye's door.

The door of the house where Skye lives. With Skye on the other side.

Holy crap. This is it.

Adrienne rings the bell.

The door opens.

Skye gasps when she sees Adrienne. "Oh, no. Did Greg—"

But then she sees me.

"You're here," she says.

"I'm here," I say.

And it begins again.

eleven

Skye

endless summer nights

BEST.

Summer.

Ever.

When Seth showed up at my door, it was like I'd opened the door to a whole new life. The kind of life I'd been waiting for. We've had two weeks of hot days on the beach and hot nights making out. I don't want this to end.

But we only have two days left.

The first thing we did this time was exchange contact info. Now I know Seth goes to Penn. I showed him where I live on a map of New Jersey. My town isn't too far from where Seth is from. I can't believe that the whole time I was growing up in Newfoundland, he was twenty miles away in West Orange. An hour from Sea Bright. The whole time I was forcing myself to be happy with the wrong boys, Seth was so much closer than I'd ever imagined. There should be some kind of radar that lets you know if your soul mate is nearby.

It all worked out, though. Fate made sure we found each other. We're going to visit back and forth all the time. Philly and Newfoundland are about one and a half, two hours apart. We can take the train on weekends. I can start driving down to Philly when I get the car my parents promised me for my birthday on November 3. We'll also have holidays.

We can totally make this work.

Not that two weeks this summer plus two days last summer equals an official relationship. I know it's too early for Seth to think of me as his girlfriend. But it feels like he will eventually. I just wish we didn't have to go our separate ways again.

Tonight is going to be epic. My parents are on the Cape. We have the whole house to ourselves. And we will be taking full advantage of it.

My new favorite place is right up here on our dune. Watching the sunset together. Being in the Now. Like most days since our reunion, we hit the beach in the morning and chilled in the afternoon. Then we split up to go home and get ready to go out. The entire night is ours.

I lean against Seth. He smells like mint and Ivory soap. He puts his arm around me, pulling me closer. I trace my hand down his other arm. Seth looks really good with a tan. His sea-glass green eyes are even more intense. He's rocking all new friendship bracelets his cousin Jade made him at camp this summer. He says he likes wearing them at college because it's a way of keeping Jade close to him. How adorable is that?

"This sunset is unreal," Seth says.

"I know. It has like every possible sunset color."

"I like watching for the second when the sun dips below the horizon. Sometimes there's a green flash."

"When I was little, I thought the sun was melting into the ocean."

"How did you explain that the next morning?"

"The ocean poured the sun back into the sky."

"Of course it did."

Seth puts an earbud in and gives me the other one. I can't remember where I've heard this song before.

"What song is this?" I ask.

"'Don't You Forget About Me.' Simple Minds. From the end of *The Breakfast Club*?"

"Yes, that movie was awesome!"

"One of the best movies ever."

We watch the sky colors blend and fade. We watch the sun sink until it's gone.

"There goes our light," I say.

"Yeah. The moon's only a waxing crescent."

"Isn't that your favorite phase?"

"No, it's waning crescent."

"What's the difference again?"

"Waning crescent goes this way." Seth draws it in the sand. "Classic. But waxing crescent goes the other way."

"So there's not much moonlight. But no worries." I take two glow sticks out of my bag. "We have glow sticks!"

"Dude."

"This one's yours." I give Seth the purple one. Then I crack the hot-pink one, shake it, and loop the lanyard around my neck.

"I don't wear glow sticks for just anyone," Seth informs me.

"I should hope not."

"That would make me a glow-stick slut."

"You're much classier than that."

"Thank you." Seth lights his glow stick and puts it on. "It doesn't get much classier than this."

A new song comes on. "What's this one?"

"'If You Leave.'"

That's all it takes for the tone to get serious. We've been pretending this summer will never end. This song is like a smack right back to reality.

> *Promise me just one more night*
> *then we'll go our separate ways*

Seth slides his fingers through my hair. "We'll see each other all the time."

"I know."

"We're not that far apart."

"It feels far."

"But we're here now."

Seth leans closer. His green eyes glitter even in the darkness. When he kisses me, all that matters is right now. Being with Seth is all I need to make me happy.

We could stay out here all night. But this is the first night we'll be alone at my house. So we force ourselves to get up and walk home. When we get to my room, there's a box sitting on my bed. It's wrapped in silver paper with a shiny pink bow.

"What's that?" I ask.

"Hmm?"

"Is it from you?"

"I have no idea."

"You rule."

"So do you. Now we've formed a club."

I dive onto my puffy white duvet and grab the box. "How did you get in?"

"Adrienne might have assisted with logistics."

"What's this for?"

"Didn't you get the memo about Just Because? It's a trendy new holiday that's taking the nation by storm."

This bow is too cute. I carefully peel its backing off the silver paper so I can stick it to my bulletin board later. When I unwrap the box and lift the lid, I can't believe what I'm seeing.

"You remembered!" I hug Seth crazy tight. "You won him for me?"

"I had to. You were meant to be together."

I lift out the plush purple unicorn. He's just as soft as I imagined.

"Thank you thank you *thank you!*"

"What are you naming him?"

"Serendipity."

"Nice."

"After this book series I read when I was little. I'm pretty sure there was a purple unicorn in one of them."

Seth's smiling all big.

"What?"

"Nothing. Just . . . I like making you happy."

I lean back against my pillows. "Then come over here."

We lie on our sides with our cheeks against the pillows, staring at each other. I've been looking forward to spending the whole night together for so long. My balcony doors are wide open. Sounds of ocean waves fill my room. The soft breeze smells like lilacs.

"Will your dad wonder where you are?" I ask.

"I told him I was sleeping over at Nick's."

"Do you even have to tell him anything, though? Now that you're like a real adult?"

"*Like* a real adult? Are you saying I'm an impostor adult?"

"It could be worse. You could be an impostor tomato."

"You lost me."

"You know how I showed you my friend Kara's site? A Day in the Life?"

"Yeah."

"She did a video on how tomatoes don't taste the way they're supposed to anymore. Most of the tomatoes in supermarkets are grown in Florida now. Which is ridiculous because Florida's soil doesn't have the right nutrients to grow decent tomatoes. And then they're picked when they're still green and exposed to this gas that turns them the perfect shade of red. So they look really good, but they have no taste."

"Impostor tomatoes."

"They are not real tomatoes."

"What a travesty."

"Kara exposed the whole racket. She got over half a million views on that one."

"Go Kara."

"She's a superstar."

"Do you miss her when you're here?"

"Yeah. And Jocelyn. But they come stay for a few days every summer. Adrienne's here, so it's not lonely or anything. And now I have you."

Seth gently presses me back against the bed. He traces his finger down my cheek.

"You totally have me," he says.

twelve

Seth

lost in love

"TRUTH OR dare?" Adrienne challenges Nick.

"Dare."

"I dare you ... to talk to that girl over there. In the red bikini." Adrienne indicates a gorgeous blonde laying out with a group near the water.

"You call that a dare?" Nick gets up from his towel. He adjusts his shades. "Give me something hard to do." He saunters over to the group, flaunting more courage in ten seconds than I've had my whole life. Except for the night I first kissed Skye. I'd never done anything like that before.

"Truth or dare?" Skye asks Adrienne.

"Truth."

"Why aren't you with Greg?"

"Skye. The Truth part of Truth or Dare is for digging up serious dirt. Not for rehashing stuff you already know."

"That's the thing. You haven't told me the whole story."

Adrienne leans back on her elbows. "My mom caught us hooking up in the pool. She threatened to ground me for the rest of the summer if I kept seeing him. What else is there to tell?"

"It just doesn't seem like you to give up so easily."

"I didn't. You know we snuck around."

"But you're not sneaking around anymore."

Skye told me all about Adrienne's guy drama. Way more than I wanted to know. Where does Adrienne's mom get off telling her daughter that the guy she wants to be with isn't good enough for her?

Adrienne gets up. "I'm going in. You coming?"

"You go ahead," Skye says. "I want to watch Nick make an ass of himself."

Adrienne heads for the water, passing Nick on the way. He pretends not to notice her. You have to admire his technique. When you're trying to impress a girl, especially a hot blonde in a killer bikini, the last thing you want to do is get caught looking at another girl.

A group of moms is kicking it old-school with a boom box. I'm pretty sure public music is against beach rules. But no one seems to care. Everyone else is zoning out with their iPods. When a new song comes on, I laugh at what I'm hearing.

"I can't believe they're playing New Kids. Nostalgia much?"

"What?"

"They're playing 'Please Don't Go Girl.' Best New Kids on the Block song, hands down."

"Weren't New Kids more like . . . a bubblegum boy band?"

I shake my head in despair. Skye has so, so much to learn. And I can't wait to teach her.

"Not exactly," I say. "I mean, yeah, their first album was bubblegummy. But they were actually really talented. Jordan's falsetto on 'I'll Be Loving You (Forever)' was exceptional. Listen to how good Joey sounds on this."

"Wow. I knew you were into eighties music, but this is serious."

"There's a hilarious clip of 'Please Don't Go Girl' live from 1988. The audience had absolutely no rhythm. They apparently existed before waving your hands in the air or clapping to a beat were invented. Joey and Jordan even crack up in the middle over the lack of clue. I'll send you the link."

Skye pulls her towel over so it's touching mine. She leans on her side, pressing up against me.

"Oooh," she says. "You're hot."

"Not as hot as Nick." We look over to see Nick killing it with red bikini girl. She's putting out all the typical signals of interest: laughing too hard, playing with her hair, posing. Nick's the kind of guy who can have a summer fling and never look back. I'm way on the other end of that spectrum. Sometimes I wish I could be more casual about girls. When guys talk about hooking up with random girls, I get how fun that could be. It's just not for me.

I watch Skye watching *The Nick Show*. She's so incredibly beautiful. What is this gorgeous girl doing with me?

"Let's go," I say. "There's someone I want you to meet."

"Who?"

"My dad." I want this thing with Skye to work. Which means getting over my embarrassment about my dad's ramshackle beach house. Skye came over the other day, but he wasn't home. He wasn't at the rink the night we went, either.

"Finally!" Skye says. "I was beginning to think he didn't actually live here."

"Oh, he lives here. He even owns a business. And you're going to freak when you find out which one."

"Which one?"

"You'll see."

"The snowball place?"

"No."

"Crab Shack?"

"No."

"Which *one*?"

"You'll see."

We get our things together. Adrienne's still swimming, so Skye goes to tell Nick to watch her stuff. My nerves are jangling now that Skye is about to meet my dad. It was different when Chloe met my dad. She kept asking when she was going to meet my parents. There was all this pressure to introduce her. But nothing feels forced with Skye. Everything just flows.

On the boardwalk, we pass the water-gun game where I won her purple unicorn.

"Anything else you want?" I ask.

"Yes!" Skye throws her arms around me, lifting off the ground and twirling. She kisses my cheek over and over. People walking by look at us.

"Making a scene again?"

"So?" Skye says between kisses.

"So it's awesome. I love when you're afflicted with sporadic bursts of spaz."

We get to the rink. This is it.

"Ready?" I say.

"For what?"

I point to the rink. "We're here."

Skye's face lights up. "No way! Your dad owns—" Her eyes darken. She stares at the neon sign.

"What's wrong?"

"Nothing. You know I love this place."

When we go in, Dad looks up from behind the counter. He's smiling all big at Skye.

"Hey, Dad. This is Skye."

"I know," Dad says. "We go way back."

At first I think he's joking. But then I see the way they're looking at each other. Like they've met before.

"Have you guys . . . You know my dad?" I ask.

"We—"

"Skye came in a while ago. We bonded over eighties nostalgia."

Skye smiles politely, rubbing her arm.

"Oh," I say.

"I didn't know he was your dad," Skye explains. "Or I would have told you."

"And I didn't know she was your Skye," Dad says. "I think that was right before you told me about her when you guys reconnected."

"It was." Skye nods emphatically.

"Well, then I guess we're past introductions!" I say.

An uncomfortable silence shoves in.

When I pictured Skye meeting my dad, I was hoping they'd hit it off right away. They'd start talking and laughing and stuff. She'd tell him how much she loves the rink. He'd dig how sweet she is. Then we'd go home and grill up some steaks. This weird vibe wasn't part of the picture.

Dad's looking at Skye. Skye's looking at the floor.

"So, um. I guess we're going," I relent.

"You two have fun," Dad says.

"Bye," Skye says.

"Nice to see you again."

As soon as we get outside I'm like, "What was that?"

"What?"

"That weirdness."

Skye keeps going down the boardwalk.

"If you guys already bonded or whatever, then why did it seem like you couldn't wait to leave? Do you not like my dad?"

"No. I mean, yes! Of course I like him."

"Then what's the problem?"

"There's no problem. Can we talk about tonight? Since it's your last night, I was thinking we could—"

"Skye. Stop." I hold her still so she has to face me. "Tell me what's going on."

"Your dad should really be the one to tell you."

"Tell me what?"

"He said some stuff. Before he knew I knew you. But I didn't know he was your dad until just now. I swear."

"What did he say?"

"He was saying how the rink reminds him of your mom. Of everything they were. He told me about when they met and how it was the best time of his life. He said he wished he could get that magic back."

"So, what, he wants to get back together with my mom?"

"Maybe. He didn't say that exactly, but . . ."

"What? Just tell me."

"It's the rink. It's . . . closing."

"For the season?"

"No. It's shutting down. Forever."

I cannot believe I'm hearing this. How can the rink be closing? Dad would never do that. Maybe she misunderstood.

"Did he tell you why?" I ask.

"He said business hasn't been good. The rink's been losing money. I guess he can't afford to keep it open."

This is bullshit. Not just about the rink. How could Dad tell all of that to a complete stranger and not even tell his own family?

"You should go talk to him," Skye says.

"No. It's my last day. I want to spend it with you."

"But—"

"Shhh." I take Skye in my arms and hug her tight. I don't ever want to let her go. But tomorrow will come. We'll go our separate ways again. Except this time will be different. This time we'll stay together.

Tomorrow isn't goodbye. Tomorrow is only see you soon.

thirteen

Skye

they say you got a boyfriend

JOCELYN HAS been trying to do these summers of reinvention ever since high school started. They never work. She always starts the summer out all optimistic, but by the middle of August she realizes there's no way. Like last summer when she tried to lose twenty pounds. Or two summers ago when she swore she'd talk to five random boys at the mall. Before Jocelyn knew it, school would be starting in three days with lots of weight left to lose and cute boys to approach. Her summers of reinvention have always massively disappointed.

Until now.

Jocelyn's summer of reinvention worked this time. She's letting her hair grow longer. It has pretty gold highlights. She lost weight. And she's determined to lose even more. Which is why Kara and I are having milk shakes while Jocelyn's sipping a lemonade. We offered to have lemonades instead, but Jocelyn wasn't hearing it.

"Diets don't work," Jocelyn announces.

Life is good. We've scored our couch at The Fountain.

Jocelyn just admitted what I've been dying for her to understand for years. Seth is coming to visit tomorrow. He's taking the last train back so we'll have as much time as possible together. I'm not even bothered that school starts next week.

"We've told you that a million times," Kara complains. "Remember my exposé on fad dieting? I did that for you."

"It got more hits than the sneezing panda," I recall.

"Yeah, I know," Jocelyn says. "But I had to try them for myself. It's not like you have to worry about losing weight. You're perfect."

Kara snorts. "Yeah, I wish. Did you see my *Flight of the Conchords* sequel?"

"It was cute!" I say. That video got some snarky comments about how lame it was and how Kara must be out of ideas. I don't get it. Why do people feel the need to spew negativity? How does being a hater help anyone?

"It was phenomenal," Jocelyn adds. "If people don't appreciate quality viewing, that's their problem."

"Dillon didn't even watch it," Kara says.

Last year it seemed like Kara and Dillon were going to break up. Kara was over sleeping with Dillon. Dillon was over Kara avoiding sex. But they love each other. They obviously want to make it work. Dillon just got back from a family vacay in Europe. Kara insists they just needed a break and that everything's fine now.

"Oh, I forgot to tell you," Jocelyn says. "I'm talking to Luke."

"You *are*?" Kara yells.

"Why didn't you tell us?"

"We're not talking yet. I meant I'm going to talk to him when we go back."

"That's awesome!" I cheer. Jocelyn's summer of reinvention was even more epic than I thought. "What made you change your mind?"

"This summer made me more confident. It's really all about changing your lifestyle. You have to take a holistic approach if you want to look better *and* feel better."

"Luke better watch out," I say. "You look amazing. Upgraded Jocelyn is in the *house*."

"What are you going to say?" Kara asks her.

"I don't know yet. I thought I'd just go up to him and see what happens."

"You should have something specific in mind. In case you get nervous."

"I'm already nervous."

"Exactly. You don't want to blow it. First impressions are everything."

"And I have a whole lunch menu planned out," Jocelyn continues, ignoring Kara. "I'm doing all healthy meals—whole wheat peanut butter sandwiches, mixed raw vegetables, salads. You guys can't let me buy anything. You know cookies are my gateway drug."

"Don't worry," I reassure her. "If you get up at lunch, I'll tackle you. Unless you're going to talk to Luke."

"We have your back," Kara says. "You have to be super careful. You could gain the weight back really quickly."

"Don't you think I know that?" Jocelyn snaps.

Kara looks at her. "No, I know, it's—"

"Didn't you hear me talking about my whole lifestyle change ten seconds ago?"

"I'm just saying that you need to be careful. That's all."

I don't know why Kara has to harsh Jocelyn's mellow. Jocelyn worked really hard to lose that weight. She's been rocking brighter colors and sexier looks. The candy-green tank top with ribbon straps she's wearing today is cut lower than anything I've ever seen her wear. She's actually feeling good about herself. Why can't Kara just be happy for her?

We need a subject change.

"What's that?" I ask Kara, pointing to the guitar pick she's wearing on a chain.

"Oh. It's from Anton."

"The lead singer of that band?"

"Persons of Interest. Yeah."

Kara did a series of A Day in the Life videos on Persons of Interest this summer. She wanted to show what life in a band was like behind the glamour. They did shows in Boston, Philly, and New York. They have a unique sound that seems to be catching on. Sort of like Coldplay on crack.

"Does Dillon know about Anton?" Jocelyn asks.

"There's nothing to know," Kara says. "Anton let me shadow him for a few days. That's it."

"But you *are* wearing his guitar pick," Jocelyn points out. "How does Dillon feel about that?"

"Dillon doesn't have to know. It's not like I'm wearing it in front of him. Anyway, we've been really happy since he got back. Happier than ever, actually."

"Speaking of happier than ever"—Jocelyn gives me wide eyes—"isn't Seth coming tomorrow?"

"Yeah," I giggle.

"Are you so excited?"

"*So* excited."

"I cannot wait to meet that boy," Kara says. She points at Jocelyn. "Prepare to have your mind blown."

"Oh, I'm prepared. We've only been hearing about him for a year."

"I'm kind of nervous," I say. "I don't want to scare him off."

"He's not going anywhere," Jocelyn soothes. "Your story is so romantic. I love how you were both thinking about each other the whole time you were apart. How you were both searching for each other at the same time? Break me off a piece of that true love."

"That's the thing. I love him. But it's like . . . how can you love someone you've only spent a few weeks with?"

"Love defies logic."

"Yeah, but if I tell him I love him this early, won't it scare him off?"

"Boys can't deal with emotions," Kara says. "Especially when they're yours and they're strong. Which I don't get. What's so scary about how we feel? Are boys so immature they can't handle anything remotely substantial?"

"I know. I want to tell Seth everything. Isn't that what you're supposed to do with your boyfriend? Share the unedited version of your lives?"

"Not this early. You'll scare him off if you tell him you already love him."

"Not necessarily," Jocelyn protests. "Seth obviously adores her. How do we know he doesn't feel the same way?"

"Have you ever heard of a boy falling in love so quickly? That's exclusively a girl thing."

"Seth's different," I say.

"But it's still better to wait for him to say 'I love you' first," Kara insists. "Guys don't like being pushed. Seth needs to feel like he's the one deciding where the relationship goes."

"Well, he kind of is. I just want to be with him. If we ever break up, it'll be because he wants to. Not me."

"There's nothing wrong with you saying 'I love you' first," Jocelyn says. "But maybe Kara's right. Maybe it is a little early to say it."

"*Maybe?*" Kara challenges. "No, it *is* too early. Trust me. I have lots of experience in this area."

"And I don't?" Jocelyn asks.

"I think I'll just go with the flow," I interrupt. "Say it when it feels right. The worst would be if it sounds forced."

"Totally," Jocelyn agrees.

Kara stays quiet. She hates when people don't accept her opinions as the absolute truth. But I wish she wouldn't take it out on Jocelyn.

✳ ✳ ✳

I can't sleep that night. All I can do is count down the hours until Seth gets here. I don't know why I'm so nervous about him visiting. He'll love everyone. Everyone will love him. Which will make it even harder when he has to leave. But we'll have the whole day together. The last train back to Philly isn't until midnight.

The next morning I'm buzzing on a heavy adrenaline/exhaustion combo. Good thing I can walk to the train station from my house. I'd be mortified if Mom had to drive me to pick Seth up. He already met my parents this summer. Which is the perfect excuse to avoid them as much as possible today. My parents love that I'm with a smart, polite boy. Not sure they're loving that he's in college. They didn't really say much when I told them about our plan to see each other every weekend. But I could tell from the looks they gave each other that they were already starting to worry.

Seth and I can ride around town on bikes once we get back to my house. Dad already said Seth could borrow his. Then a new friend of Kara's is picking us up for a party. I cannot *wait* for Seth to meet Jocelyn and Kara.

I get to the train station early. The warm breeze transports me right back to that night we spent together in Sea Bright. The waves crashing in the distance. The soft breeze on our skin. All alone with Seth in my room, kissing him late into the night. I'm dying to spend the night with him again. We might get a chance when I visit him if he can get rid of his roommate.

A train whistle brings me back.

He's finally here.

Seth sees me before he gets off the train. He waves at me through the windows as he walks toward the exit. I'm bouncing and laughing and waving back.

When Seth steps down onto the platform, I notice that he's carrying a delicate blue flower.

"For you," he says, holding it out.

"Thank you."

He kisses me over and over. I vaguely hear the train pulling away. A few car doors slam in the parking lot. And then it's just us.

"How was the train?" I ask, breathless.

"Not so bad. I almost missed the transfer. But the Universe was on our side. It went pretty fast."

"What did you do?"

"Whipped out my usual train reinforcements. Book, music, sketchbook."

"I love reading on the train. That or staring out the window listening to music."

"There's something so relaxing about watching all the houses go by."

"I know."

"So," Seth looks around. "This is where you live. It's really . . . green."

The Newfoundland train station is pretty desolate. We're surrounded by trees. The train tracks disappear into the woods in both directions. A dirt road leads out from the little parking lot. Houses are spread so far apart that the nearest one is half a mile down the road.

"You were warned there's not much here but woods and more woods."

"And you." He kisses me again. Then he notices the little rundown train depot. "That's not open, is it?"

"No, it closed down a long time ago. But there was a guy who used to live there."

"In *there*?"

"It was weird."

"Is there even plumbing?"

"I guess so. He lived there for a while."

"What happened?"

"No one knows. He just left."

Seth goes over and tries to open the door. It's locked.

"Ready to go?" I say.

Seth shifts his bag to his other shoulder. He holds my hand. "Ready."

When we get home, I'm relieved to find a note from Mom saying that she's out with Dad. She added that she's looking forward to seeing Seth again.

"Let's go to my room," I say. My heart is pounding as we climb the stairs. I can't believe Seth's finally going to be in my room. All those nights last year wishing I could find him. Remembering what it felt like to be with him. Replaying our night together on the beach. And now he's here.

"Wow," Seth says when he sees my room.

"This is it."

"Yeah it is. It's so you."

I watch him explore my room, looking at pictures and picking things up. His fascination makes me feel like I'm seeing everything for the first time, too. My room looks a lot like my room at the summer house. They're both big with lots of windows. They both have walk-in closets. Except instead of a balcony facing the ocean, here I have a picture window with a bench. The bench has adorable vinyl pillows I found at a boutique in the city that say things like PEACE and LOVE.

Seth is looking at everything on my dresser. The red metal Love statue replica. My glitter pens with the fuzzy feathers. The Marimekko tin pillbox that I have no idea what to put in it but was so cute I had to buy it. Flower Post-its and the tooth eraser I got at the dentist's when I was seven and the I ♥ Earth keychain everyone in One World got last year and the sparkly confetti I saved from the roller rink and just everything.

"I'm going to get a vase for my flower," I say. "Be right back."

Seth is transfixed by my rings in their bamboo container. When I come back, he's over by my bed. I try to breathe normally.

"This flower is so pretty." I put the vase on my windowsill.

"It reminded me of you. Or you remind me of a flower."

"I do?"

"You totally do. You both like lots of natural light and water and fresh air." He comes over and hugs me. "And you smell good."

I giggle.

"And I was hoping . . . I wanted to ask you if . . . would you be my girlfriend?"

"Of course."

"Awesome."

Part of me wants to stay in my room all day with Seth. But he wants to see my town. And I really want to show him everything. So we go get the bikes out of the garage and ride around for a few hours. We stop by Green Pond. I show him my school. Then we go to The Fountain for gelato.

"Whoa," Seth says.

"This place is the real deal," I confirm.

"No, it's . . . remember I told you about my job? At the soda fountain?"

"Yeah."

"That place is Phantom Fountain. This is The Fountain."

"Whoa."

"That's what I said."

These annoying little kids are hogging my couch. We get our gelato to go. We eat it outside, watching a random muskrat cross the street. Then we ride home to get ready for the party. As soon as I open the door, Mom is upon us.

"You're back! We've been waiting for you. Hi, Seth. It's nice to see you again."

"Thanks for letting me visit, Mrs. Davis."

"You kids must be hungry. Dinner's almost ready."

I throw Seth a look. My eyes say, *Sorry about this. I thought we could avoid the whole family dinner thing.* His eyes say, *No worries. Your parents are cool.*

We've barely started eating when Dad begins interrogating Seth.

"So, Seth. I understand you're at Penn."

"Yes, sir."

"Excellent university. I'm a Princeton man myself."

"Oh." Seth nods warmly in recognition, the way people who've attended fancy colleges do with each other.

"What are your career goals?"

"I'm a business major."

"Wharton!"

Seth nods.

"That will open lots of doors for you. What area of business are you interested in?"

"Colin, let him eat," Mom says.

"No, it's okay," Seth tells her. "I'm not exactly sure yet. It's still . . . new."

"Well, you'll figure it out. The important thing is that you're getting a quality education. I'd love to go back and do college all over again. It's a priceless experience."

Seth nods, but I know what he's thinking. There's a huge price tag attached to his college education. Seth's dad told him that he had to get a job to help pay for college this year. The semester just started and it's already stressing him out. He doesn't like to talk about it. But I can hear it in his voice when we talk every night. He's exhausted.

The doorbell rings.

"That's our ride," I say. "We have to go."

"Have fun!" Mom says.

"Drive safe," Dad adds, even though neither of us is driving.

When I open the door, Kara takes one look at Seth and smiles.

"Hi," she says. "I'm Kara."

"Seth."

"I *know*. Welcome."

On the way to the car, Kara keeps slapping my arm and making these *ohmygodhe'samazing* expressions. I slap her back to stop slapping me before Seth sees.

Kara gets in the front. Seth and I climb in back.

"Where's Jocelyn?" I ask.

"She's meeting us there. Guys, this is Chanel."

"Hey," I say. "Thanks for the ride."

"No problem."

Chanel is the one who invited Kara to the party. They met this summer after Chanel contacted Kara about a video she did for A Day in the Life. Kara did this whole thing on the transition from high school to college. Chanel wanted to collaborate with Kara on a follow-up piece she was working on for her filmmaking class. Kara couldn't resist. She'd never pass up the chance to meet a fan.

When we get to the party, it's clear I'm out of my element. It's at this big, old house a few of Chanel's college friends are renting. This house reminds me of the professor's house in *Wonder Boys*. Even though it's packed with people, it kind of has a cold, empty feel. Kara waves to someone she must have met through Chanel. They take off, leaving us lingering awkwardly by the door.

We don't know anyone else here. It's an eclectic group—frat boys, intellectuals, old dudes who probably enjoy smoking pipes. A guy who looks like he's in college stops to talk to us.

"Do you know Chanel?" I ask him.

"Who doesn't know Chanel? Her short film on global species extinction was a masterpiece."

"What college do you guys go to?"

"Montclair State. We're in the New Jersey School of Conservation."

"Cool," Seth says. "So you're a professional environmentalist."

"Trying to be. Not the easiest job when almost everyone is determined to destroy the planet."

Seth turns to me. "You should check out that program."

My heart sinks. I was hoping he'd want me to go to college in Philly. Or at least a lot closer to Philly.

"I don't know," I say. "I'm not sure what I want to do yet." I don't know what I want to be, but I know what I *don't* want to be. Typical. Average. I want more from my life than to sleepwalk through the expected motions. I want my life to really mean something. I want it to be amazing. It would be perfect if my career involved the environment in some way. But as soon as I decide exactly what I want to do, I'll be one step closer to narrowing down college choices. Colleges that might be far away from Seth. That's a step I'm not ready to take.

"What about you?" Environmentalist Guy asks Seth.

"I'm a business major at Penn."

"Really? You don't seem the type."

"Why?"

"You have a creative vibe. I'm not getting corporate suit from you at all."

"You're right. I'd rather be an art major."

"You should switch," I say. I keep trying to convince him to switch majors. "You should be majoring in what you love."

"I would if it were an option."

"Why isn't it an option?" Environmentalist Guy asks.

"That's a long, boring story. Basically it comes down to—"

"You're here!" Jocelyn shrieks, running up to us.

"Hey!" I'm so happy to see her. "Jocelyn, this is Seth."

"Yay!" Jocelyn cheers. Seth sticks out his hand to shake hers. She hugs him instead.

"Sweet, I needed a hug," Seth says.

"And this is . . ." I gesture toward the guy we've been talking to.

"Dale," he says. "Good to meet you."

Kara comes over with Chanel and some other people. She glances at Jocelyn.

"Uh, *hey* Kara," Jocelyn says with tone.

For a second it looks like Kara's about to attack. But then she gives Jocelyn a weak smile and starts talking to Dale. I wonder what that was about. Maybe it's just leftover tension from yesterday.

We end up talking for a long time. Jocelyn focuses on Seth, finding out all she can about him without being overwhelming. Or trying not to be overwhelming. For a person who's normally shy around boys, she's really hitting it off with him.

I'm stoked that Jocelyn and Kara are finally meeting Seth. I love being out as a couple. I love talking to strangers as a couple, putting myself out in the world as Seth's girlfriend. But I can't wait to be alone with him.

Seth leans over to whisper in my ear. "Want to get out of here?" he asks.

"Totally." I break Jocelyn away from the group. "We have to go," I tell her. "Seth has to catch his train."

"I thought it was at midnight."

"Yeah, but . . ." I glance at Seth. My face gets hot.

"Oh. *Oh*. Yeah, no, I'll tell Kara. Go before they force you into beer pong."

"You. Rule." I hug Jocelyn goodbye. We're about to leave when Kara comes running over.

"Wait! Are you guys leaving?"

"Yeah, we have to go," I say.

"How are you getting home?"

Good question.

"We'll grab a ride to the train station," Seth says.

"Here, I'll go out with you. One of Chanel's friends is outside. He can take you."

"Nice," Seth says. "Actually, I'm going to hit the bathroom. Be right back."

As soon as Seth goes down the hall, Jocelyn and Kara snap into full-on gush mode.

"Oh my god he is *so* hot." Kara.

"Those *eyes*." Jocelyn.

"Those eyes take you to a whole other realm of existence. How can you even remember your name when he's talking to you?"

"I love how cute he is with you! You guys are perfect together."

"Did you see how he couldn't stop touching her all night?" Kara asks Jocelyn.

"I know! And how he looked at her?"

"Like he couldn't get enough."

"I dream about a boy looking at me that way," Jocelyn sighs.

"Which Luke will when you start talking to him," I say.

"Really?"

"Totally. Right, Kara?"

Kara nods a little, glancing around the room.

"Wow," Jocelyn says. "Is it really that hard for you to be supportive of me?"

"What?"

"You can't even be happy for me?"

"Happy for what? Nothing's happened yet."

Jocelyn glares at Kara. Kara glares back. I'm trying to figure out how to smooth things over when Seth returns.

"Let's get you that ride," Kara says, still glaring at Jocelyn.

I give Jocelyn a questioning look. She just shakes her head.

Outside, Kara asks Seth if she can borrow me for a minute. We walk across the yard.

"Sorry about all the awkwardness with Jocelyn," she says.

"What happened?"

"Just more of the same drama. I don't know what her problem is."

The last thing I want to do is have Kara rant at me about Jocelyn when my last hours to be with Seth are ticking away. So I just say, "I'm sure you guys will work it out."

"It's hard to be supportive when she's being so delusional."

"What do you mean?"

"Does she really think she's going to talk to Luke? After all this time avoiding him?"

I glance over at Seth. He's looking up at the stars.

"I hope so," I say.

"Anyway. Let's get you back to your hot boyfriend."

Kara hooks us up with Chanel's friend. He's cool about giving us a short ride to the train station. Even better—our train's coming in ten minutes. We snuggle up on a bench to wait.

"The Universe is on our side again," Seth says.

"It always was."

We stare at each other, contemplating the serendipity of it all. Then we make out until the train comes.

Our train car is empty. The conductor saunters down the aisle to take our tickets. The door closes with a *clickbang* when he leaves. I slide over to the window seat and put my legs over Seth's lap. But the armrest is digging into my back. I look around to make sure no one else is in our car. Then I straddle Seth so I'm facing him, squeezing his thighs between my legs.

"Hi," I say.

"Have we met?"

"I don't think so. I'm Skye."

"That's a pretty name. You're a pretty girl."

"You're kind of forward for someone who hasn't introduced himself."

"I wish to remain anonymous. It's hotter that way."

"Done."

"So what do you do for fun?"

"Other than climb up on cute boys on trains?"

"I thought everyone did that."

"I enjoy long walks on the beach at sunset."

"Sounds romantic."

"Oh, it is. What about you?"

"I am very romantic as well."

"Give me an example."

"Well." Seth slides his hands around my waist. He pulls me closer. "Making out on trains is romantic."

"Is it? Where's the mood lighting? Where's the music?"

"Sorry, the conductor didn't get the memo. I ordered that stuff ages ago."

"That's what you get for taking the discount train."

"But the discount train offers privacy." Seth glides his hand down the back of my hair. I lean into him.

By the time we get to our stop, Seth's hands are under my shirt and my lips feel so used I don't know how we're going to get past my parents without them knowing what we've been doing. But we are stealth. We sneak past the living room, where they're watching TV. We escape to my room.

"How much time do we have?" I ask, closing my door.

"Eighty-two minutes."

We get on my bed. Clothes come off. Time disappears. It feels like we've only been making out for five minutes when Mom calls up to me from downstairs.

"Skye? We need to get Seth to the station or he'll miss his train!"

No way. There's no freaking way over an hour just passed.

I'm not ready to let him go. And hello, Mom's totally going to be able to tell what we've been doing in here this whole time. Gah!

"Coming!" I yell down.

"This sucks," Seth says.

"I know."

We scramble to get dressed. I check myself in the mirror above my dresser. My hair looks like it's been professionally tousled for an edgy photo shoot. My lips are red and puffy. I actually look kind of hot.

Mom does not need to see me looking any kind of hot.

"Skye!" she yells up the stairs. "Let's go!"

"We're *coming*!"

Seth comes up behind me. He wraps his arms around my waist. I lean back against him. We look at each other in the mirror.

"I don't want to go," he says.

"I don't want you to go."

"But you're coming to visit me next weekend. And we'll talk every night."

"I miss you already."

Seth turns me around for one last kiss. As his lips touch mine, I already feel how empty this week is going to be without him. Time will stretch out endlessly. I'll be dying to feel him close to me again. So I try to be in the moment as much as I can, focusing on this kiss. It's the last part of him I'll have until next time.

fourteen

Seth

that thunder in your heart

OF COURSE Astor dumped Grant last year. Right after the Diner on the Square incident.

Getting dumped hit Grant hard. He was in denial at first. Stomping around all like, "How could she dump *me*? How backward is that?" Then he crashed. He didn't get out of bed for a week. When Grant finally emerged (and, thankfully, took a shower), I started to notice little changes. He didn't rant so much about how our society is rotting from the inside out. Some of his pretentious edge was softened. Eventually he just . . . chilled.

I'm finding the less conceited, mellower version of Grant to be way more likable.

We have the same suite as last year. Grant isn't the only improvement. Dorian has actually—wait for it—stopped gaming. He was put on academic probation last semester. When Dorian's parents found out he was on the verge of being kicked out of the Ivy League because he couldn't tear himself away from his controller, they came down with the wrath of people paying for his inordinately expensive existence. They threatened to cut him off entirely if he didn't shape up.

Dorian needs a 3.0 this semester or they're kicking him out. He decided to go cold turkey. He left his gaming gear at home.

Things have changed for me, too. I didn't say anything to Skye because I didn't want her to worry. Which she definitely would if she knew how hard this semester has been for me. Working plus classes equals way less time to see Skye. All I want to do is be with her. If I could make a career out of being with Skye, I'd be all set.

Unfortunately, that's not my job. I'm a soda jerk at Phantom Fountain. It's this old-school soda fountain on Pine and Twenty-first. My dad knows the owner. Guess he called in a favor. I knew less than nothing about serving ice cream when I started. My job involves making sundaes, providing couples with two colossal straws for the black-and-white milk shakes they share, and mastering the seltzer machine. I'm still perfecting my egg cream skills.

Vern is one of the old guys who's been a regular since the creation of ice cream. He samples the fresh egg cream I place in front of him.

"Not bad," Vern says. "Not bad at all. You're learning."

"Thank you." I wipe the counter and quickly check the clock. Almost quitting time.

"Got that big date tonight, huh?" Vern says with a knowing wink. Everyone and their dog knows Skye is coming to visit. I can't help it. She's all I can think about.

"I do."

"What do you like about this girl?"

"Ever just click with someone, Vern?"

Vern stirs his egg cream. "I seem to remember something like that."

"Then you know."

"Don't go breaking any hearts."

"No, sir." I check the clock again. "She'll be here soon. I better get moving."

"Have some extra fun for me, hear?"

"Sure thing."

We shake on it.

In the break room, I throw my paper cap in my locker. I change shirts and shove my work shirt in my bag. There's no way I'd wear it in public. It's a vintage-style collared white shirt with black piping that has my name embroidered above the pocket. The shirt is dorktastic in here. But out in the real world it's just dorky.

Skye was supposed to visit last weekend. Our original plan was to visit each other every weekend, switching back and forth. But last weekend I had to work a double. Plus I had to cram for this killer Corporate Finance exam. My classes aren't as simple as I thought they'd be. There were only a few classes that really challenged me in high school. I was expecting college to be more of the same. But a couple of these business major classes are kicking my ass. Maybe it would be different if I found any of this crap interesting.

Between studying for exams and writing papers, dedicating every weekend to Skye won't be easy. It feels like I haven't seen her in a million years.

I remember last year when I couldn't stop thinking about Skye. Wondering where she was. Wondering what she was doing. How I'd hoped she would show up and find me one night.

Now my fantasy is reality.

I race across the bridge back to campus. There are so many things I want to show Skye. But I didn't want to overwhelm her by planning too much. I want her to want to come back. She told her parents she was spending the night in a girl's room in another dorm. A girl Skye said was my friend, but doesn't actually exist. I'm sure they suspect she'll be staying in my room.

In my bed.

Grant swore he'd find somewhere else to sleep tonight. He'll probably crash with Tim and Dorian. Now that Dorian's on gaming hiatus, he's turning out to be a decent guy.

No one's at the suite when I get back. Which is perfect. I don't have time for distractions. I have an hour before Skye's train gets in. That's enough time to take a shower, clean my room, and dash back down to the station to pick her up. Barely. Good thing I washed my sheets last night.

Someone knocks as I'm drying off after my shower. I tuck the towel around my waist and answer the door.

Skye is here.

"Hey!" I say. "I thought I was picking you up."

"I caught an earlier train. I could not *wait* to get here. Is that okay?"

"Of course it's okay! It's more than okay."

"Awesome."

"I'm in a towel."

"I can see that."

"Come in."

Skye surveys the room. She puts her bag down on my bed. "This is obviously your side."

"Gee, how could you tell?"

"Oh, I don't know. Absence of grossness? Does Grant ever clean?"

"Not so much, no."

Skye makes a face at his side of the room. "Isn't that a health hazard?"

"We're boys." I open the window some more. "Boys are kind of health hazards in general."

"You're way less hazardous."

"I try. So, um, let me just . . ." I grab clothes out of my dresser. "I'll get dressed. Make yourself at home in my luxurious four square feet of space."

"I'll yell if I get lost."

When I come out of the bathroom, Skye's in front of my easel, looking at the collage I'm working on. I'm using a big piece of wood I found in a construction site discard pile. Construction workers are usually pretty good about letting me take whatever they're getting rid of.

"Is this the one you were telling me about?" she asks.

"Yeah."

"It's gorgeous."

"Thanks."

"I love the colors."

"Did you notice the blue?"

She looks again. "Which blue?"

I move behind her and point to the blue. "This one here."

"It's pretty."

"Does it remind you of anything?"

"Hmm..."

"I mixed it to match the color of your eyes. Or I was trying to." As soon as the words leave my mouth, I want to snatch them back. Is she going to think that's cheesy? I hold my breath.

Skye turns around to face me. "That's, like, the sweetest thing anyone's ever done for me," she says.

"Really?"

"Really."

"I missed you." I pull her against me. I never want to let her go.

"I missed you more."

I kiss her gently. This is the way I used to imagine kissing Skye in my fantasies where she suddenly appeared after searching for me. She'd tell me how she couldn't stop thinking about me. How she knew we were meant to be together. How I'm the one she wants to be with forever. Then we would—

The bathroom door whips open.

"Oh sorry, man," Tim says. "I was looking for Grant."

"This is Skye."

"Hey." Tim does an awkward wave thing. "I've heard a lot about you."

"That must have been pretty boring," Skye says, blushing from getting caught.

"Seriously? This guy thinks you're the bomb diggity shiznit."

"Um. Thanks?"

"I'll leave you guys alone, but do you know if Grant's staying with us tonight?"

"He might be. I'm not sure."

"No prob, I'll catch up with him later. Good to meet you, Skye."

"You too."

The bathroom door bangs shut.

"Want to have dinner in Center City?" I ask. "There's tons of stuff I want to show you. But if you don't feel like walking back down again, that's cool."

"No, I took a cab here."

"Oh." Must be nice. I never take cabs. They're too expensive.

Whenever I walk to campus from the train station, an intense feeling floods over me. It's like this strong sense of coming home. Crossing the Walnut Street Bridge to Center City is powerful, too. If freedom, excitement, and possibility all got together and decided to become an emotion, that would be the feeling I get. By the time I hit

Rittenhouse Square, I'm buzzing over the potential awe-someness of it all. Growing up in suburbia will do that to you. One whiff of city life and you're like an uncaged animal running wild.

Crossing the bridge with Skye is a whole different thing. That intense zing still hits me. But it means more now. I want to share this part of my life with her in a way I've never wanted to with anyone else. I wish I could explain exactly how this makes me feel. It's really hard to get someone as excited about your own routine places as you are. She'll never know exactly how much this affects me. But I still want to try to explain.

"See down there?" I point down the steep staircase that leads from the Center City end of the bridge to my peaceful, leafy future. "That's where I want to live next year. Around Twentieth and Pine, to be exact."

"Can I see?"

"I thought we'd go by tomorrow. The place where I work is right near there. Vern wants to meet you."

"Who?"

"You'll see."

We turn right toward Locust Street. Showing her Ritten-house Square is a good way to start. She'll think it's cute.

"What's Wawa?" Skye asks.

"It's like a 7-Eleven. Dude! Let's go in. There's something you have to try."

I hold the door open for her. Then I dart to the Tastykake rack.

"You have to try these." I grab a pack of Butterscotch Krimpets. "They will change your life."

"Before dinner?"

"They will change your life after dinner."

"Sold."

"Are you thirsty?"

She nods.

"Water?"

She nods again.

I pay for our waters and the Butterscotch Krimpets. I'm a big spender like that. I've actually been saving up for this dinner. Skye keeps talking about these trendy restaurants she wants to go to. Of course they're the most expensive restaurants in Center City. I don't know how to tell her that I can't afford them. But what I could see when I looked them up online is that Skye digs intimate restaurants with low lighting. So I came up with three places I can sort of afford that I think she'll love. We'll go wherever she wants.

"Aw, this is so cute!" Skye says when we get to Rittenhouse Square. The square is this oasis surrounded by busy streets. Quaint benches line pathways that divide grassy sections. People are sitting on the grass in groups or just relaxing on their own. "Do you come here a lot?"

"Not as much as I used to. But yeah, it's fun to bring my sketchbook and just people watch."

"Can we sit for a minute?"

"Of course. Whatever you want."

We grab a bench by the fountain. I put my arm around

Skye. She leans against my shoulder. It's starting to get dark. We watch the building lights come on.

"Are you beyond excited to get an apartment next year?" Skye says.

"You have no idea."

She sits up. "I'm pretty sure I do. I can't wait to be free. You're so lucky. I still have a whole year left."

"And then I can stay at your place."

"I'll probably have to live in the dorms freshman year. Isn't that standard?"

"Yeah, but it's better. You don't really get the full college experience if you live off campus right away."

"Does it bother you that I'm still in high school?"

"What? No. Where did that come from?"

"You can't sleep over in my room."

"So? You can sleep over here."

"I can't come see you whenever I want."

"Neither can I. Anyway, between school and work, I'm not exactly enjoying an abundance of free time these days."

"All these things are happening to you that I don't even know about yet. The 'full college experience.' I can't relate to what you're going through."

"Hey. Skye?"

"Yeah?"

I hug her close to me. "I don't care about any of those things. I just want to be with you."

"Promise?"

"Promise."

Right when I kiss her, the streetlamp above us blinks on. Skye looks up at it and laughs.

"Of course," she says.

"Let's go. We're having appetizers."

"Sounds classy."

"Oh, it is."

I take her to the Palomar. The Palomar is a chic hotel near the square. Their restaurant has a lounge where you can order snacks. Karen and I discovered it one night when we were exploring. What I really wanted to do was rent a room here tonight. But then I saw the prices. There was no way.

The hostess seats us on big, square cushions. Our little table has a candle. Mood lighting is in full effect. I remember how they keep dimming the lights as it gets later. By the time they close, you can hardly see who you're leaving with. Which might be the idea. There's a connecting bar.

I order the truffle popcorn.

"Popcorn?" Skye asks.

"Trust me. This isn't just any popcorn. It's the best popcorn ever. It melts in your mouth."

"Wow. That's some serious popcorn."

"Serious deliciousness."

"This place is awesome." Skye looks around at the sleek bar, the lit mosaic, the hipster crowd. "How did you find it?"

I was hoping she wouldn't ask me that. Karen is the last thing I want to talk about. I've learned that nothing good comes from talking about ex-girlfriends with new ones. But Skye is different. Maybe she won't care.

"There was . . . I was with someone. This girl Karen. For a little while."

"For how long?"

"A few months."

"Was it . . . serious?"

"No."

"Why did you break up?"

"It wasn't fair to her. I wanted to be with you the whole time."

Skye smiles. "You did?"

"Of course."

Our popcorn arrives.

"You ready for this?" I warn.

Skye takes a piece of popcorn. She's not expecting much as she puts it in her mouth. But the truffle decadence instantly rocks her world.

"Oh my god," she says. "Can we just have five bowls of this for dinner?"

"That would be badass."

"This is the best thing *ever*."

"I know." And it's only four bucks.

We talk about classes and friends and last summer. Skye is stressed out about some drama between Kara and Jocelyn.

"They're acting even weirder than before," she says. "I usually love hanging out with them. But it's like every time we're together, they put me in the middle of their . . .

whatever it is." Skye takes some more popcorn. "I hate that things are this awkward. Getting together used to make me so happy. I really miss that."

Skye tells me about this altercation yesterday where Kara said stuff and Jocelyn did stuff. The details are blurry. Catty girl drama makes me tune out. I try to focus. But my mind keeps going back to our earlier conversation. Now that Skye knows about Karen, I'm wondering if she was with anyone this past year.

I don't want to know.

I have to know.

"So . . . what about you?" I venture. "Were you seeing anyone?"

"When?"

"This past year."

Skye nods. "Ben. It wasn't serious, either."

"Did you break up with him?"

"Yeah. Right before spring break."

"Why?"

"Because he wasn't you."

Dude. Where has this girl been all my life?

The restaurants I picked out for dinner are all within five blocks of one another. I take Skye to each one so she can look at their menus posted outside. She picks the one I thought she would.

We both feel like staying out after dinner. So we go exploring Center City. She shows me things I'd never noticed before, like this desolate alleyway with little doors along the wall. I make a mental note to find out what those doors were for.

"This is amazing," Skye says on South Street. One wall of a building is covered with tiles in all different shapes and colors.

"I knew you'd love it."

"Being out late rules. We could stay out all night if we wanted to."

"We could."

"That rules!"

"But it probably wouldn't be the safest." *Aaand* the award for the biggest reject goes to me. Could I be any lamer? I just wouldn't want anything to happen to Skye, wandering around some of these sketchy streets at three in the morning. I'm not exactly anyone's first choice as a bodyguard.

We walk back to campus after some more exploring. As we're crossing the bridge, I'm filled with that same sensation of coming home. It would be perfect if I could do a copy/paste of this feeling into Skye's heart. But being able to walk with her is almost as good.

Eminem is blasting from one of the frat houses on Locust Walk. Locust Walk goes down the middle of the main campus. It's the nicest part of campus during the day. But it's annoying on weekends. Frat boys lug couches and lounge chairs and TVs out onto their front lawns. They kick back to watch everyone with an air of entitlement. I heard one guy actually make oinking noises when a girl passed by. We were going in opposite directions. Her eyes met mine when the oinking happened. She rushed past, staring hard at the ground. I glared at the oinking dumbass. He gave me one of those smug nods like, *Yeah, I'm the man. You're welcome.*

Weekend nights are even worse. Frat parties rage full force. Packs of skankily dressed girls flock to them.

"Let's crash that party," Skye says.

"What?"

"Over there. Is that a frat?"

"We don't do frat parties."

"Which is exactly why we should. Come on!"

Skye drags me to the frat house. Maybe she's right. Going to this party could be fun in an ironic sort of way.

The whole place is lit with black lights. Everyone's wearing white shirts. It looks like they used neon paint to draw on their clothes and skin.

"It's a highlighter party!" Skye yells over Beyoncé.

"What's that?"

"Everyone draws on each other with highlighters! Too bad we're not wearing white!"

Parties aren't fun if you don't know anyone. These two drunk guys are running around randomly graffitiing people with highlighters. We really don't feel like getting drawn on, so we sit on the floor by the couch. It's like having our own private mini party while the big party swells around us. There's something about being at a cheesy frat party with the music blaring and the bass thumping and Skye crushed up against me that's surprisingly sexy. I need to be alone with her.

"Can we go now?" I yell over Rihanna.

"Only because we're not wearing white."

I'm hoping Grant will be out for the night. When we get to my room, he's hastily cramming stuff in his bag.

"Oh hey!" he says. "I was just leaving."

"This is Skye."

"Hey Skye, how are you?"

"Good."

"Good, good." The deodorant Grant tries to throw in his bag flies across the room. "I'm just—I'll be out of here in a sec."

Way to be subtle, bro.

"Are you dazzled by our fine institution of higher learning?" Grant asks Skye.

"It's . . . impressive," she says, trying to avoid looking at his side of the room.

Grant hefts his bag over his shoulder. "See you tomorrow. But, you know, not too early or anything," he tells me with a pointed look.

Grant's attempts to communicate subtext are an epic fail. You'd think he was more nervous than me about a girl spending the night in my bed.

"I'll just let myself out," he says.

"Later, man."

We're finally alone.

Is it dorky that I made a mix for tonight? Bruce Springsteen comes on first with "She's the One." My heart is pounding at what might happen.

"So . . . do you . . ." I try to keep it casual. "Are you tired?"

"Kind of." Skye's getting clothes out of her bag. "You?"

"It's hard to tell. The excitement of you being here is overpowering everything else."

"Aw." Skye kisses me. "I'll be right out." She takes some clothes and a zippered pouch with hearts all over it into the bathroom. The shower turns on.

Should I get changed? I usually just sleep in my boxers and maybe a T-shirt if it's cold. Or should I stay dressed? I decide to lie on my bed and flip through Grant's copy of *If You Meet the Buddha on the Road, Kill Him!*

When Skye comes out, she's wearing a cute little pink tank top and striped pajama shorts. She takes her hair clip out. Her hair flows like honey over her shoulders. She smells like fresh air.

"What are you reading?" she asks.

"One of Grant's philosophy books."

"Are you getting into philosophy?"

"It seems more appealing now that he's not a ranting d-bag anymore."

Skye laughs. She lies next to me on my bed.

"Hey," she says.

"Hey." I put the book down. "You look really pretty."

"Thanks."

I slide my fingers down her arm. "Why's your skin so soft?"

"Is it?"

"Yeah. It's like . . ." I brush my hand against her cheek. There are no words.

Skye reaches under my shirt. She rubs her hand down my back. "You should take this off."

I immediately sit up and whip off my shirt. Led Zeppelin's "All My Love" comes on.

"Are you trying to seduce me with love songs?" Skye teases.

"What if I was?"

"Then I would have to say it's working."

I'm not exactly sure when it gets light out. There's a good chance we just set a new world record for making out. Skye only has on her bra and lacy underwear. I'm down to my boxers. We obviously want to keep kissing forever. But at some point we must have fallen asleep. We're on top of the covers, me on my back, Skye on her stomach with her head on my chest and one leg bent over mine, when Grant barges in.

"Whoa!" he yells.

I jolt awake, register what's going on, and yank the blanket over Skye.

"Didn't see anything," Grant says.

Your roommate jolting you awake while your half-naked girlfriend is sleeping on top of you is not the best way to wake up.

We stayed up until at least sunrise. So of course it's twelve thirty now. Which means we barely have time for brunch before Skye has to catch her train. She uses the bathroom first. When I come out after my shower, Skye and

Grant are sitting on my bed, laughing at something on his laptop.

"What's so funny?" I ask.

"I'm showing Grant A Day in the Life," Skye says. "Kara just posted a video on Shit High School Seniors Say."

"This," Grant proclaims, "is my new favorite site."

"Yay."

"Here." Grant takes his laptop over to his desk. "I'm following her right now."

"Sweet!"

"Ready to eat?" I ask Skye.

"I could *not* be hungrier."

We go to Diner on the Square. Which Skye loves. Because even though she has expensive taste, she also appreciates unpretentious quality. Then I walk her to the train station and sit with her on the platform. I don't want her to have to wait alone.

Saying goodbye is the hardest thing I've ever had to do.

"Remember," Skye says, "it's not 'goodbye.' It's 'until next time.'"

I just wish it could always be next time.

fifteen

Skye

your life is on fire

MY PARENTS want to talk to me. They didn't say what about. Just that we need to talk.

I don't have a good feeling about this.

"We wanted to check in with you," Mom starts. She's sitting next to Dad on the couch. I'm bracing myself in the big chair. "It feels like we haven't talked in a while. How's everything going?"

"I'm fine, Mom."

"We've noticed that you're spending a lot of time talking to Seth. And all those visits—"

"We haven't seen each other in three weeks!" I hate that I can't see Seth more. We were supposed to see each other every weekend. But between extra work shifts on his end and college app madness on mine, our weekends are packed. The last time I saw Seth was before Halloween. It's tragic.

"You talk for hours every night," Mom says. "We're concerned that you're neglecting your schoolwork. Your first marking-period grades weren't what they should be."

"I'm getting my grades up. I got an A on my history quiz! Everyone else got like a C."

"There are college applications . . . and your volunteer work . . ."

"Remember what happened to the Farley kid," Dad mumbles ominously.

"I'm not going to have a nervous breakdown, Dad. And I'm getting my college apps done. Seth has nothing to do with any of this."

"We think he does, sweetheart," Mom insists. "We know how important Seth is to you. It's natural for you to want to see him more often. Now with the car . . . we want to make sure your priorities are in order."

My parents gave me an Infiniti for my eighteenth birthday. It's silver and has a sunroof. I love it. I love having the freedom to go wherever I want. Theoretically. In reality, I just want to drive down to see Seth every day.

"Trust me," I say. "I'm getting everything done. You guys can stop worrying."

"It would have been nice to include One World on your college applications for this year," Dad says.

"Except One World had a weekly time requirement. Which is why I do Safe Rides now." Quitting One World wasn't my finest moment, but Seth and I are trying to make more time to see each other. I would feel selfish giving up volunteer work entirely, though. Which is why I joined Safe Rides. Drivers can spend as much time as they want giving rides to teens to get them home safely. "It's way more flexible. Isn't that what you guys want? For me to not do too much while still doing everything?"

Mom sighs. She looks at Dad for help.

"Couldn't you go out with a boy from school?" he blurts.

"Dad. Seth is my *boyfriend*."

"We know he is," Mom interjects. "What your father's trying to say is . . . well, it would be easier if you had a boyfriend who lives here. You wouldn't have to spend so much time traveling."

"Are you guys serious? Do you really think it works like that? If I were interested in any of the boys at school, I'd be with one of them. Seth and I belong together. I *love* him."

Mom gives Dad a frightened look.

"I know what goes on in those dorm rooms," Dad throws down.

"Seth has three roommates. And it's not like I'm sleeping over in his room or anything. I told you. I stay with his friend." I don't want to lie about any of this. It's just that they'd never let me visit Seth if they knew I was staying in his room. "You can't stop me from seeing my boyfriend."

"That's not what we want," Mom says. "We're concerned about you, Skye. We want to make sure your priorities are in order."

"My priorities haven't changed. I'm still the same person." I can't remember the last time I was so furious at my parents. Part of me wants to yell all the things I'm keeping inside at them and storm out. But I have to make them understand how much Seth means to me. I'd die if they didn't let me see him. "I get that you're worried about me. But I'm fine. Really. Seth makes me happy. Which makes everything else in my life better."

"We're happy for you, honey," Mom says.

"You've always trusted me before. Are you saying you don't trust me now?"

"There's no need to twist things around," Dad says. "Of course we trust you. You've never given us a reason not to."

"Good. Because Seth and I want to go on a road trip Thanksgiving weekend. It would really be sad if you stopped trusting my judgment. I'm eighteen now. I'm an adult." I search my parents' eyes for compassion. "Please let me go. Let me prove to you that you can always trust me."

Mom gives Dad a sad smile. He nods. I know what they're thinking. I'm going to do what I want with Seth. Trying to stop me will only make things worse. They have to let me go, whether they want to or not. It's time.

"We'll need to discuss logistics," Mom says.

"Totally."

"We have to know where you are at all times."

"Absolutely."

"You have to promise to pick up when we call."

"Done."

"Well. We'll think about it."

That means yes. I can't wait to tell Seth. I'm relieved their interrogation is over. Good thing I'm going out with my girls tonight. I'd hate to be trapped here with the parents watching me, tiptoeing around all the things we didn't say.

Later when Jocelyn and Kara are in my car and we're driving into the night, I'm waiting for my stress to melt away. There's nothing like chilling with your best friends to mellow you out. Except when tension has been building between them for so long that you're worried they're about to explode any second.

"How'd it go with Luke last night?" I ask Jocelyn in the rearview mirror. They just started going out. Jocelyn went up to Luke pretty soon after school started, just like she said she would. Kara could not have been more shocked. I was double happy when Jocelyn started talking to Luke—happy that they might finally get together, but also happy that Jocelyn proved Kara wrong. I didn't like the way Kara was talking behind Jocelyn's back, saying that Jocelyn was never going to approach Luke. They'd been talking for almost two months when Luke asked Jocelyn out a few days ago. She was happier than I've ever seen her.

"It was kind of a disaster," Jocelyn admits. "Luke forgot that he had plans with his friends. So I was like, 'No problem, we can reschedge.' But then he kept saying how he wants me to hang out with his friends sometime and I was all, 'I'd *love* to meet your friends!' Which could not have been more awkward because then of course he had to invite me along even though I was clearly horning in on boys' night. Why didn't I wait until he asked me to hang with them? Why did I have to throw myself at them like that?"

"But was it okay once you guys were out?" I ask hopefully.

"Not so much. Luke didn't tell them I was coming. It was so obvious I wedged myself into their plans. Which made me super uncomfortable and nervous and I kept apologizing for everything. We were at the rib joint and one of his friends stepped on my foot at the table and I was like, 'Sorry!' when I wasn't even the one who stepped on someone's foot. Who *was* that? It's like Luke's bringing back all the insecurities I worked so hard to overcome. Welcome back to square one. May I take your order? We have a humiliation special with a side of mortified."

I feel Jocelyn's pain. She's in that frustrating/euphoric/traumatic new relationship phase of uncertainty where all you want to do is impress the boy. Even if it compromises who you are. Even if it turns you into someone you don't recognize. Why do girls get like that? It's like we'd rather be who we think the boy wants us to be instead of actually being ourselves.

Kara would normally give Jocelyn some advice right about now. But she's not saying anything. She just keeps staring out the window.

The strip mall at the edge of town is only good for one thing: the totally random, totally delicious pommes frites place. If there's one thing we love, it's crispy fries with fifty kinds of dipping sauce. We get all set up with large cones of fries and a bunch of dipping sauces and dig in.

Kara's phone buzzes. She takes it out of her bag and laughs at the screen. She frantically texts back.

Jocelyn shoots me an exasperated look. Kara's been ignoring us for texts a lot lately. We usually tell each other who it is. But Kara's not telling us anything. Sometimes it seems like she'd rather be talking to whoever's texting her than hanging out with us.

"Who are you texting?" Jocelyn asks.

"Chanel. She wanted to come tonight, but she couldn't make it."

That's news to us. Since when is Chanel part of our group? And since when do we invite other people without asking if it's okay first?

Kara keeps texting. Jocelyn and I eat our fries in the ominous silence.

"Your fries are getting cold," Jocelyn tells Kara after a few long minutes.

"Sorry." Kara finishes with her phone. She leaves it on the table. "She was asking about Dillon."

"Did you guys make up yet?" I ask.

"No. I don't even know why we're fighting. So what if I went to see Anton's show with Chanel instead of him? Dillon doesn't even like Persons of Interest."

That post-separation happiness cloud Kara and Dillon were floating on didn't last long. They keep getting in fights about what Kara insists is nothing. Expect it's not nothing. It's a boy Kara is clearly fighting feelings for, even if she won't admit it.

Jocelyn says, "If you have feelings for Anton—"

"The only feelings I have are annoyed ones. Dillon thinks he's entitled to dictate who my friends are. It's getting old."

"He's worried about Anton."

Kara's pomme frite freezes halfway to her mouth. "What?"

"Dillon's jealous of Anton," Jocelyn clarifies.

"Why should he be jealous? Anton and I are just friends."

We look at Kara.

"I'm allowed to be friends with a boy," Kara says defensively. "Last time I checked, it wasn't illegal."

"It's okay if you like Anton," Jocelyn says.

"I don't! I'm in love with Dillon, in case you haven't noticed."

"Actually? I haven't."

"What's that supposed to mean?"

Jocelyn shakes her head. "Forget it."

"No, what?"

"It's just that . . . all you guys do is fight. The only time you sound happy is when you're talking about Anton. You obviously like him."

"You don't know what you're talking about," Kara fires back. "You've only been with Luke for three weeks. That's nothing. Dillon and I have been together for three *years*."

"Why does everything have to be a competition with you?"

"No, it doesn't."

"Yes, it does! You always have to be better at everything. Or more experienced or more informed or more *whatever*. Just because I have less relationship experience than you doesn't mean I don't know what I'm talking about."

"*Outburst*. See, this is why I've been hanging out with Chanel. She doesn't pick stupid fights with me."

"Maybe you're the reason people are fighting with you."

Jocelyn told me about how Kara's been increasingly getting on her nerves, but she's never told Kara to her face before. I'm not exactly sure why it's coming out now. I guess when you're carrying so much weight around, you never know when it might get too heavy to keep carrying.

"What's all this about?" Kara asks.

"It's about how you can be really insensitive sometimes." Jocelyn's voice is shaky. "You have this attitude like the whole world revolves around you. Why do you have to control everything?"

"Like when?"

"Like when you didn't want Chanel to drive me to that party because you just *had* to be the first one to meet Seth. Or how you always take the passenger seat like you own it. Did it ever occur to you that I might want to sit up front?"

"Um . . ."

"I'm sorry I've been keeping all this in. But I'm not sorry for saying it. When I made a pact to do senior year differently, one thing I promised myself is that I'd speak up more. So this is me speaking up."

Kara looks at me like, *Can you believe this?*

I concentrate on digging the crunchiest fries out from the bottom of my cone.

Obviously, we don't feel like doing anything else. The ride home is a nightmare. Kara and Jocelyn stare out their windows in icy silence.

Kara gets dropped off first. She opens the back door. No way was she calling shotgun after what Jocelyn said. "I'll call you tomorrow, Skye. You probably have a lot you want to tell me without . . . you know. Certain people in the car."

"Like she would take your side?" Jocelyn says. "Anyone could see how ridiculous you're being."

"She doesn't think I'm being ridiculous. She's my friend."

"So was I until you turned into a megabitch!"

"Can you please tell her she's the one being a bitch, Skye?"

They both look at me expectantly. How am I going to handle this? Should I agree with both sides? Or pull a Switzerland and remain neutral?

"You guys," I say. "Don't put me in the middle of . . . whatever."

"Whatever?" Kara says. "One best friend turning against me and the other refusing to defend me is not *whatever*." She heaves out of the backseat, slams the door, and stalks across her lawn.

I drive to Jocelyn's house. The lump in my throat won't go away.

"You agree with me, right?" Jocelyn asks.

"Can I . . . I really don't want to get stuck in the middle," I say. "Sorry if that sounds lame."

"No, I completely understand," Jocelyn says. But I can tell she's disappointed I'm not taking her side.

After I drop Jocelyn off and head home, a crying fit attacks out of nowhere. One minute I'm planning my strategy to stay out of their fight until Jocelyn and Kara make up. The next minute I'm pulling over to the side of the road. I'm crying too hard to keep driving.

I call Seth when I can breathe again.

"Hey," he says. "I was just thinking about you."

"I'm having a meltdown."

"What's wrong?"

I tell Seth everything.

"That sucks," he says.

"I hate all this stress. We used to be best friends. When did everything start sucking so hard?"

"When we weren't looking."

Seth is awesome for being there for me, listening to me rant. But enough about me.

"How did your statistics paper go?" I ask.

"Nailed it."

"Seriously?"

"No. More like scraped it together three minutes before class. I was channeling those losers in high school who pumped the font up to twenty-four points to meet page requirements."

"I'm sure it wasn't that bad."

"Oh, it wasn't. It was worse."

I laugh.

"Finally!" Seth shouts. "You've never made me work so hard for a laugh before."

"Sorry."

"No apologies. I'm always up for a challenge. You know what?"

"What?"

"I can't wait for next weekend."

"Same here." I haven't seen Seth in forever. Next weekend is our road trip.

"Your parents are so cool for letting you go. How'd you pull that off?"

"We were talking and it came up. I think they need to prove

that they can still trust me. Oh, and my mom will be calling me every five minutes. Just so you know."

"Sounds romantic."

"Right?"

"At least we don't have to launch Plan B." Plan B was telling my parents that some of Seth's friends were staying at one of their family's cabins in upstate New York for the weekend. The girls would get the bedrooms and the boys would sleep in the living room. We were hoping it'd be one of those lies my parents would forget about after the trip. But I was nervous about lying. It was an elaborate plan with huge potential for blowing up in our faces.

"Well . . . I guess I should let you go," I say reluctantly. Hanging up with Seth is always impossible.

"Until tomorrow."

"Okay. I love you."

Oh. My. God.

Did I really just tell Seth I love him? Is that what I said? Wasn't I waiting until the time was right?

I hold my breath, waiting for Seth to say it back.

"Bye," is all he says.

"Oh. Um. Bye."

What. Was. *That?*

sixteen

Seth

forever's gonna start tonight

EVER SINCE the I Love You, I've been all twarked up in a ball of stress.

I love you. How hard is that to say? Why didn't I say it back?

Of course I love Skye. I've loved her since the first second I saw her. When I met Skye at that beach party, it felt like my real life was finally starting. I just knew we were meant to be together.

And now she loves me.

Skye said "I love you" and I was too much of a neurotic freak to say it back. The thing about saying "I love you" is that there's no going back once you say it. The potential for Skye to hurt me would increase drastically if I told her how much she means to me. Trusting that we'll make this work isn't easy. But it's what I have to do if we're going to move forward.

I have to say it back.

But when? Calling her and blurting it out would be lame.

It has to be soon, though. Relationships are doomed if you let too much time go by after the I Love You without saying it back.

Wait. Our road trip would be the perfect time. There will be several ideal scenarios to choose from:

Scenario 1—We get a hotel room the first night. I surprise Skye by setting up the room with tons of candles. It's all romantic. I say it.

Scenario 2—We stop at one of those scenic overlooks. Skye is impressed with the view. I say it.

Scenario 3—We wake up together at the same time. Skye is glowing in the morning light. I tell her she looks beautiful. I say it.

None of those scenarios plays out on the road trip. Here's when I actually say it:

We're at a rest stop stocking up on supplies. While Skye is in the bathroom, I quickly buy a few things for tonight. Then I hide the bag in my coat pocket and gather some snacks. I grab a pack of Ho Hos.

Skye comes up behind me. She puts her hands over my eyes. "Guess who?" she whispers.

I turn around. I look at her. And it just comes out.

"I love you," I say. "I've loved you since the first time I saw you."

"Really?"

"Of course."

"When you didn't say it back—"

"That was stupid. I should have said it back."

"So I can stop worrying."

"You have me," I reassure her. "You'll always have me."

Skye hugs me tight. I hug her back, still holding the Ho Hos. Not exactly one of the ideal scenarios I pictured. But this is perfect in its own way.

I'm relieved it's my turn to drive. I felt like such a loser when we took off from Skye's house this morning in her car. How pathetic is it that I don't even have my own car to take my girlfriend on a road trip? I'm hoping to make up for it tonight. This is the first time I've seen Skye since she turned eighteen. I wanted to do something special for her birthday. Which is why there will be a few surprises at the motel later.

This whole day has kind of been one surprise after another. Skye is a big fan of going with the flow. She makes me want to be more spontaneous. When we made plans for this road trip, we agreed that we'd be flexible. We'd do whatever we felt like. It's been awesome so far. We drove to this pottery house in upstate New York. Skye wanted to get a special flowerpot there for her mom's Christmas present. Then we went to the Delaware Water Gap. It's cool how the massive dip of that valley cuts out a U-shaped piece of sky. We had fun hiking and taking in the views.

Skye is navigating the map while I drive. We just crossed back into New Jersey.

"We're near Hope," she says.

"Hope who?"

"No, it's a town. My parents used to take me to the Land

of Make Believe there when I was little. I thought it was the best amusement park ever."

"Better than Great Adventure?"

"That was before my Great Adventure days."

"Dude, I love Great Adventure. Isn't it near Sea Bright? We should drive down there tomorrow."

"Don't they close in October?"

"Drat."

"Drat? Really?"

"Ironically."

Skye studies the map. "I wonder what it's like in Sea Bright right now."

"Cold."

"September is the latest I've ever been there. We used to make a big fuss every year when we closed the house for the season. My cousins and aunts and uncles would come down for that last weekend. We'd cover all the furniture with drop cloths, eat everything left in the kitchen, play games. The grownups would tell stories we'd heard a million times already. But it wasn't cheesy. It was awesome." Skye has a faraway look, remembering. "We haven't gotten together like that in a long time. Everyone's so busy now."

"Do you want to drive down?"

"No, you're right. It's freezing. And the house is closed. Anyway . . ." Skye puts her hand on my thigh. "I'd rather stay in a hotel."

I glance at her. Her eyes burn into mine.

Is this happening?

Whenever I think about having sex with Skye for the first time, we're usually in some tricked-out place. My ideal scenario would be to rent a room at the Palomar. Not just any room. Their deluxe king suite. Affording the room is never an issue in my fantasy. Which will probably never become reality, given that the only thing I've been able to afford at the Palomar is their four-dollar truffle popcorn. But it's all good. There are other options. Like kicking Grant out for the night and transforming my room into a Skye-friendly paradise.

The way she's squeezing my thigh makes me think we might not get back in time to explore that option. Maybe packing those condoms wasn't just wishful thinking.

This road trip isn't about destinations. It's about driving around with absolute freedom. The best part is knowing that we can do whatever we want, whenever we want. So we get lost for a while, just driving around. We blast the road trip mix I made. Skye sings along to "My Sharona." She knows more of my favorite eighties music now, plus a lot of late-seventies classics like this one. As if I wasn't impressed already.

After dinner at the Waffle House (did I mention I was a big spender?), we find a motel off Route 80 called the Starlight Inn. I've been racking my brain for how to set up the room without Skye knowing. I really want her to be surprised. But there's no stealth way to get ten minutes alone in our room first.

I pay for the room with a wad of fives and singles. The crusty guy behind the counter counts my bills.

"Tips," I explain to Skye.

"Nice."

"So, um . . . I kind of need the room for a few minutes. Before you come in."

"Okay . . ."

"It's a surprise."

"A surprise?"

I nod.

"For me?"

I nod.

"You're so sweet. I'll wait here." Skye takes her bag over to a couch that's seen better days.

Crusty counter guy leers at her.

"I'll be back in a few minutes," I announce loudly enough for him to hear.

Skye loves confetti. That was clear our first time at the roller rink. I take out a big bag of confetti from the party store and fling it all over the bedspread. I put two sparkly birthday party hats on the table with the gift I wrapped and rewrapped about twenty times before it looked decent enough. Then I unwrap a pack of Hostess Strawberry CupCakes and put a birthday candle in hers. She said these were her favorite one time at Wawa. I leave the cupcakes on the wrapper because I forgot plates. The box of mini candles I bought when we stopped at the Go

Mart was a genius purchase. I put candles all around the room. I remembered to bring matches for Skye's birthday candle, so I quickly light the mini candles and turn out the light.

Crusty counter guy frowns at my return to the lobby.

"Come on." I reach for Skye to pull her up. There's a definite possibility she'll think her late birthday party sucks. But Skye's face lights up when she sees the room.

"This. Is awesome," she says.

"You don't think it's lame?"

"No way. How could confetti and party hats—are those strawberry cupcakes? This is the opposite of lame." Skye goes over to her present. "You didn't have to get me anything. Those flowers were gorgeous."

The last guy I was going to be was the loser who can't see his girlfriend on her eighteenth birthday and then doesn't give her anything on top of it. I sent her a huge bouquet of flowers on her birthday. It came with chocolate and a fuzzy stuffed penguin. Sacrificing a few nights out in Center City with Grant and Tim and two weeks of coffee from the Good Karma Café to save up for the flowers was worth it. Skye called me right after she got them. Hearing her go all happy girl on me was sweet.

"Can I open it?" Skye asks.

"Of course."

She unwraps her gift. She pulls out the small box I decoupaged with tropical images. The inside is lined with purple velvet. I found a shade of purple that almost matches the couch she likes at The Fountain.

"I love it," she says.

"It's for shells and things from Sea Bright. I know you like collecting little things there. This way you won't lose them."

"It's beautiful. It feels like . . . me."

Score. "Ready to make a wish?"

"Always." She sits at the table and puts on her party hat. She holds the other hat out to me. "Party hat up."

I put on the party hat so its pointy top is sticking out sideways. Then I light her candle. Skye looks at me while she makes a wish. When she blows out the candle, I clap.

"Hope your wish comes true," I say.

"Oh, I'm pretty sure it will." She picks up her pink cupcake. "I can't believe you remembered these. You and your Tastykake obsession."

"You can't deny their deliciousness."

"You could deny it if you had horrible taste."

"You have excellent taste."

"Duh. That's why I'm with you." Skye comes over and sits on my lap. She puts her arms around my neck. "Can I just say this is the best birthday party ever?"

"Yes, you can."

Skye kisses me. She straddles the chair, her thighs tight against my hips. The kissing gets intense. Way more intense than it's ever been.

This is happening.

After all my planning, after imagining all those ideal scenarios, our first time is going to be in a cheap motel room. But this reality is so much better than all those fantasies.

This is how I know I can trust Skye. She doesn't care that our first time isn't at the Palomar or some other perfect place. She just wants to be with me. Which is all I need to know.

seventeen

Skye

where do we go from here

OF COURSE I can't wait to see Seth. It's just that if I were any more exhausted, I would be driving off the road. My eyes keep trying to close. A car honked at me a few miles back. I have a scary feeling I might have been swerving into the next lane. You're supposed to pull over and take a nap if you're this tired. People die this way. But I'm so exhausted that if I took a nap I'd wake up two days from now. Then I'd have to turn around and go back home without seeing Seth.

There's some gum in my bag. I stuff two pieces in my mouth and chew them with vigor. I blast Seth's latest mix. "The Safety Dance" perks me up. I roll the window down all the way, letting the crisp March wind smack against my face. Why did I leave so late? I wasn't even doing anything. When I got home from school I packed, then kicked back in my room, then we had dinner. The next thing I knew it was almost eight.

Familiar landmarks soothe me as I get closer to Penn's campus. The big University of Pennsylvania sign over Walnut Street makes me smile. Not just because I'm about to see Seth. This will be my reality next year. Hopefully I'll be going to college right here in Philly. Seth and I will see each other every day. We'll have friends from both colleges to do things with. Weekends will be all ours to own the city. We'll chill in coffeehouses in the afternoons and have romantic grownup date nights. Philly has some of the best restaurants. I want to try them all. Every Saturday night we could do dinner and see a movie or play after.

Next year is going to rule.

I park in the lot at Thirty-eighth and Walnut. By the time I get to Seth's dorm, it's past ten. He looks relieved to see me when he comes down to sign me in.

"Sorry, I left late," I explain.

"Are you okay?" Seth asks.

"Yeah. Just tired."

"Then let's get in bed. We can watch a movie if you want. I'll make popcorn."

"Awesome."

The first thing I notice in Seth's room is the picture we took in front of the Love statue last time I was here. Seth has it in a silver frame on his desk. Which soothes me even more.

I take my pajamas into the bathroom to change even though Grant's not here and Seth has seen everything. The first thing I do is lock the other bathroom door that leads to the connecting room. I'd die if those guys barged in on me. The whole shared bathroom thing is probably the worst part of college. That, and getting stuck with a disgusting roommate like Grant who never cleans his side of the room. I didn't want to say anything when I came in, but it's getting worse.

I come out in my pajama bottoms with the tiny hearts and a matching tank that says L'AMOUR. Seth said how cute they were last time I wore them.

"Movie selections," Seth announces. "We have *I Love You, Man*; *Up in the Air*; and *Whip It*. Your choice."

I choose *I Love You, Man*. It's one of the few movies both girls and boys enjoy equally. Well, almost equally. I'm sure Paul Rudd is more entertaining for me to watch. He's supercute for an old guy.

We're into the movie at first. But we don't finish watching it. Which is basically how it's been since we started sleeping together four months ago. It's like we try to do other things, but all we really want to do is have sex. Maybe it would be different if we saw each other all the time. We've only had a few nights together since our road trip. I wasn't expecting to lose my virginity at a place called the Starlight Inn. But it was perfect. Seth was perfect.

Kara kept telling me the first time is not the best. She was right about it hurting a little. But being completely in the moment, feeling how much Seth loved me, I was swept away by the intensity of it all. I'd never felt so connected to another person in my whole entire life.

Having sex in Seth's dorm room is more complicated than it was at the Starlight Inn. First off, Grant could come in anytime. Seth tells Grant when I'm going to be here and Grant is always good about sleeping over somewhere else, but it's still his room. Plus Dorian and Tim usually have people in their room. You can only lock the bathroom doors if you're in the bathroom. So there's always a chance that someone might come barging in from their side.

Another thing that bothers me is how dingy this room is. Grant's side is so gross. Does he ever clean? Or do laundry? It was pretty ripe in here all winter with the window closed. Lately it smells like dirty socks and boy sweat. I know it isn't Seth's fault. Grant is the grody one. Seth always tries to make his room more appealing. When he lights the cinnamon-scented candle on his dresser, turns out the light, and starts kissing me, it's like we're instantly transported to our own private world. But I miss the total privacy we had at the Starlight Inn. It would be awesome if we could spend every weekend at a hotel.

The movie's still playing when I get up to go to the bathroom. Apparently, I'm still lost in our dreamy private world because I forget to lock the other door.

Dorian busts in. While I'm on the toilet.

I scream. I only bothered to put on my bra and panties since I was going right back to bed. Both of which are entirely exposed to Dorian. Who keeps gawking at me.

"Get out!" I yell.

He snaps out of it, slamming the door behind him.

"You okay?" Seth calls.

"Yeah, just a sec." The dreamy private world has vanished. Now I'm annoyed.

When I open the door to Seth's room, the warm, romantic atmosphere from before is gone. The room feels stark and cold. I get a whiff of dirty-laundry smell hovering under the cinnamon. The stench brings back my headache from the drive. Why do I always have to be the one to come here so we can spend the night together? If we got a hotel room, we could meet halfway in between. Driving four hours round-trip to be with Seth was fun at first. Now it's getting old.

I hate that I'm still in high school. I hate that we can't live together yet. I hate that Seth can't come to my house without my parents getting all up in our business.

All I want to do is be with Seth. All the time. But it's like, what are we doing? This long-distance thing sucks. We hardly see each other. We basically have a relationship over the phone. It's like we're spending more time with the fantasy versions of each other instead of the real us.

"What happened?" Seth asks when I get back in bed.

"Ick. Dorian walked in on me."

"What?"

"It was my fault. I didn't lock the door."

"No, he should have knocked. What a dumbass. Did he see anything?"

"Just me peeing."

"Oh, man. Sorry about that."

"I've been through worse," I say. Even though I can't remember what was worse than having my boyfriend's suitemate ogling me on their filthy toilet. Seth doesn't need to know that it took a few seconds for Dorian to look away. They had enough drama last year over Dorian's gaming addiction. I want to keep the peace.

"Here, snuggle up," Seth says. He pulls me to him. The dreamy private world comes back a little.

"What do you want to do tomorrow?" he asks.

"Hmm." There are tons of fun things to do in Center City. Even hanging out around campus can be fun. But I can't think of anything specific I feel like doing. "Not sure yet. Too tired."

"Let's sleep. You'll feel better tomorrow."

I'll feel better when I know where I'm going to college. I'll feel better when I can live closer to Seth. And I'll totally feel better this summer. Only three more months till freedom. I cannot. Effing. *Wait*. Memories of Sea Bright float through my mind, warping and blurring as I drift off to sleep.

"This summer is going to be amazing," I mumble.

Seth stays quiet.

"Right?" I ask.

"Um . . . I don't know if I'll be able to go to Sea Bright this summer."

I'm suddenly wide awake.

"Why not?"

"I applied for an internship in Chicago. It's for the whole summer."

"What? Why didn't you tell me?"

"I wasn't going to tell you until I found out if I got it."

Our summer together in Sea Bright was the one thing I was looking forward to the most. And now it might not happen? And what's this about an internship? Seth never said anything about applying for an internship.

"Where's the internship?" I ask.

"At the Art Institute of Chicago."

"I didn't know you were thinking about art internships."

"I wasn't. I mean, Grant's been talking to me about changing my major next year—"

"Seriously?" I sit up. I've been trying to convince Seth to switch to art forever. He never listens. But now Grant tells him and he wants to? "You didn't tell me you were changing your major."

"This is all new, Skye. This all just happened a couple weeks ago."

"Why didn't you tell me?"

"I'm telling you now. I haven't seen you in a while and . . . I don't know. It never came up on the phone."

How can all this stuff be happening to Seth without me knowing about it? It's like I don't even know him anymore. If I applied for an internship or was thinking about changing my major, Seth would be the first person I'd want to tell. Why doesn't he feel the same way?

I really don't want to be like this. All nagging and interrogating Seth about why he didn't tell me. But I can't help it.

"So you might go to Chicago this summer," I reiterate.

"Yeah."

"For the whole summer."

"If I get the internship."

"Why didn't you apply anywhere around here?"

"The deadlines had passed for most of the internships I wanted. There wasn't anything local left to apply for."

Visions of our perfect summer together shatter before my

eyes. Am I horrible for hoping he doesn't get the internship?

"Hey." Seth reaches up to rub my back. "This is a really good internship. It could help me a lot if I change my major to art."

"Well then. I hope you get it."

"I'm sorry about the summer. But I probably won't even get it. We'll be back in Sea Bright just like you wanted." His tone is calming, but I can hear a hint of sadness.

The edge of Seth's blanket is frayed. A zigzaggy thread is sticking out. I pinch it between my fingers. If I pulled this thread, how long would it go? Would his whole blanket unravel?

Trying to fall asleep to the sounds of rowdy boys in the other room and Seth's breath on my neck, I wonder what's going to happen to us.

eighteen

Seth

if only i'd thought of the right words

CAN SOMEONE explain how we went from blissed-out lovesick territory to unrelenting tension overnight? Because I didn't see this coming. At all.

Skye was fine when she got here last night. Everything was amazing. But then she came out of the bathroom and it was like she was a different person. She said she was tired. I thought she'd feel better in the morning.

Not so much.

Brunch at Diner on the Square was strained. We didn't have our usual pep and zing. When Skye doesn't bring the pep, I can't bring the zing. Even the walk back to my dorm wasn't comforting like it usually is.

"Why do you put up with that?" Skye gestures to Grant's side of the room.

"That's how Grant is. He's not going to change."

"But aren't there rules about cleaning your room?"

"Not that I've seen." Talking about Grant isn't what

I want to be doing with Skye right now. We still have the room to ourselves. If she doesn't want to go anywhere, we should be taking advantage of the privacy.

Skye sits on my bed next to her bag. She wrinkles her nose at a dirty bowl on Grant's desk. "Have you ever said anything to him?"

"No."

"Why not?"

"Because I can't control him."

Skye rummages in her bag.

I sit down next to her. "What's wrong?" I ask.

"Nothing. I told you. I'm fine."

"Except you're not fine."

She shrugs.

"So why are you telling me you're fine?"

"I'm fine, okay? I'm just figuring out when I should leave. My parents have been insane and I have a ton of homework. And the drive is *so long*."

"Look, I'm sorry you have to do all the driving. But it's not like we can spend the night in your room anyway."

"Why can't we get a hotel room?"

"Where?"

"There are some nice hotels like twenty minutes from my house. You could take the train and I could pick you up at the station and drive us."

"I can't afford to pay for hotels all the time."

"I'll pay."

"I don't want you to pay. I don't have time to take the

train up anyway. Putting myself through college means I can't just take off work whenever I feel like it. This isn't high school."

"Excuse me?" Skye gets off the bed. "What does high school have to do with it?"

I really didn't want to get into this. Skye has no idea what I'm going through. I should have known this would happen that first night in Sea Bright, looking up at those massive houses on the hill. She can't remotely relate to how worried I am about money. Saying she'll pay for hotel rooms? Can't she see how degrading that is?

"You just . . . you don't understand."

"Try me."

"Your parents are going to pay for college, no question. You can't imagine what it's like to have to work all the time. I hate having to say no to concerts and dinners and things that I'd rather be doing because I don't have the time or money."

"So you're mad at me because my parents have money?"

"No. I'm just saying that things aren't as simple as they used to be."

"You're right. You used to care about what I said."

"What are you talking about?"

"How many times did I say you should drop business and major in art? I tried convincing you so many times to follow your heart. But now Grant tells you and you're doing it?"

"It was easy for you to say. You never have to worry about money."

"What does money have to do with majoring in what you love?"

"Some of us can't do whatever we want!" I yell. "You're always going to be taken care of. It doesn't matter what you major in or what you decide to do with your life. You never have to worry about surviving. But I'm not as lucky."

Skye leans against the door, crossing her arms tightly.

"You just . . . have these expectations. I can't do whatever you want." My head is screaming at me to shut up. Too bad I'm not listening. "Even just going out to dinner and a movie means I'm broke for a week after."

"I said I'll pay!"

"No, that's not—I *want* to be able to take you out. When you told me about how you want to go out every weekend next year to all those expensive restaurants and plays . . . I'd love to be able to give you those nights. But I hope you'd be equally okay with just hanging out."

"You're acting like my life is perfect. I also have problems, in case you didn't notice."

"What, like Kara and Jocelyn being in a fight? How much longer are you going to let that drag on?" Kara and Jocelyn got in a huge fight right before our road trip. They haven't talked to each other since. Skye's been dividing her time between them. Every time we talk on the phone, she complains about being stuck in the middle of that stupid fight. Classic high school bullshit. They could make up tomorrow if Skye pushed them.

"You think I have control over them? They're the ones who got in a fight. They're the ones who put me in the middle."

"You can choose not to be in the middle anymore."

"How?"

"Tell them to get over it. Don't girls usually make up like two days after saying they hate each other?"

"Um . . . *no?*"

"Why put up with unnecessary drama?"

"This isn't unnecessary drama. This is my friends in a fight that will apparently never end. You know how stressful it's been for me. Why can't you be more supportive?"

"I have been supportive. I'm supportive every time you complain about it. It's just . . . I've got bigger things to worry about than some high school fight. Some of us have real problems."

Skye blinks at me. She grabs her bag.

"Yeah . . ." she says calmly. "I'm gonna go."

"Please don't go. I didn't mean to—"

"No. Really. I need to leave."

And then she's gone.

nineteen

Skye

we've got to make it last

WHEN THE same group of loud girls piles into the back of my car like they did last weekend and the weekend before, I know I'm over Safe Rides.

Don't get me wrong. Safe Rides is an excellent service for drunk kids who shouldn't drive and for kids who have no other way to get home from parties. But there are so many other kids who get ridonculous wasted knowing I'll be there to take them home. I see the same kids being stupid every weekend. It's sad that their idea of fun is getting so drunk they can't stand up. Then hurling in some bushes.

I'm not psyched to be driving these three girls home. They enjoy screaming about how they're going to throw up in my car. Which I've luckily been able to avoid so far. Tonight the loudest, most obnoxious girl has a problem with me.

"So, like, you just drive drunk kids home? Instead of getting drunk yourself?" She tries to make eye contact in the rearview mirror.

"Pretty much."

"Because you're an uptight bitch?"

The other girls find this hysterical. One of them is laughing so hard she starts making retching noises.

"Do you need me to pull over?" I ask.

"No, it's okay," she slurs unconvincingly.

"Do you ever drink?" obnoxious girl presses me.

"Not really."

"*Not really* as in you sometimes do, or *not really* as in never?"

"Drinking isn't really my thing."

"Oh! It's not your *thing*! Hear that, ladies? Our driver here thinks she's superior. I wonder how superior she'd be if I hurled all over her floor?"

"That vomit smell never leaves," the third girl intones.

"Just tell me if you need me to pull over." Why did I switch from One World to Safe Rides again? I could be painting an Earth Day poster right now.

Ever since that big fight I had with Seth three weeks ago, I've been throwing myself into school and activities and friends. Anything to take my mind off what's been happening with us. Which I know is wrong. I should be trying to fix us. It just got too exhausting. We still talk, but not every single night like we used to. And we don't stay on the phone as long. It's like we're pretending everything's fine when we both know it's not. I still don't understand what happened. Why was I so mean to him? All this baggage I didn't even realize I was dragging around suddenly split a zipper and burst open. Something snapped in Seth's room that night. I used to feel like nothing could ever come between us, like the bond we have could never be broken.

Now I'm not so sure.

I said some harsh stuff. But so did Seth. He made me sound like a conceited princess who never has to worry about anything. He has no idea how stressful my life is right now. That whole thing about senior year being a breeze? Is only true about classes. Getting into college is a whole other issue.

My first college acceptance wasn't an acceptance. It was a rejection. From Penn. I knew Penn was a long shot, but I had to at least try to get in. My grades aren't bad or anything. They're above average. They're just not Ivy League material. I didn't tell Seth I was applying. I didn't want to feel even worse about myself when I had to tell him I didn't get in.

Then I was accepted to Drexel and Philadelphia University. I was stoked. Those colleges are close to Penn. I'm still waiting to hear from Temple, which is about half an hour from Penn. Drexel's campus practically touches Penn's campus. It sucks that I would have to live in the dorms my first two years, but I could go over to Seth's anytime. Things would be so much better if we could be together every day. So going to Drexel seemed like the best solution.

But then. I got accepted to New York University.

NYU was never part of the plan. I mostly applied to colleges in Philly. But the college advisor convinced me to apply to some really good colleges in case anything changed. Even though I told her nothing was going to change with Seth.

Only . . . things have changed. I've changed. I used to think Seth was all I needed to make me happy. Now I realize I need more.

There's a big difference between NYU and Drexel. NYU is a much better college. How am I going to feel four years from now after I've graduated from Drexel and I'm ready to start my career and the person who went to NYU gets picked over me for the job I want? Of course being with Seth is important. Of course I want to be with him every day. But I have to think about other parts of my life, too. Plus NYU is in New York City, which is way more exciting than Philly. Seth and I wouldn't be that much farther away from each other than we are now.

I also got into San Diego State. In California. Which would be like starting a whole new life.

I haven't made a decision yet.

After I drop the girls off at their houses, I drive over to Green Pond. Some kids from One World are having a bonfire. I could really use a s'more. Or twenty.

Jocelyn waves me over. The big, soft blanket she always uses for outdoor activities is spread out right near the bonfire. I sit down next to her.

"Did everyone get home safe?" Jocelyn asks. She always asks this after a Safe Rides shift.

"The important thing is that my car survived."

"What happened?"

"Remember those idiot girls who had a burping contest last time?"

"Thanks, I was trying to forget them."

"So was I. Until they threatened to hurl in my car again."

"Evil skanks."

"I think I'm done with Safe Rides."

Jocelyn gasps excitedly. "Please say you're coming back to One World!"

"Maybe. I don't know. It's so late in the year."

"But we need help with our Earth Day fund-raiser. And everyone misses you. *I* miss you."

"Ha." I nudge Jocelyn like she's joking. She looks serious. "What's up?"

"I know I see you all the time. But I was sad when you left One World. That was our thing."

"We have lots of things."

"Not like One World. Not where I could count on seeing you for a little while every Thursday. It made me so jealous when you and Kara would do stuff without me, or when you'd call her instead of me. It made me feel like something in our friendship was missing."

"Wow. I had no idea you felt that way."

"Yeah, well. I didn't say anything because I felt like a loser. It seemed like you were better friends with her than me."

"That's ridiculous!"

"I know."

"You know we'll always be BFFs, right?"

"Always."

Jocelyn looks over to where Luke is playing soccer with some other guys. He catches her looking and smiles. She blows him a kiss. Jocelyn is so happy with Luke. I wish I'd known that she felt bad before, though. I would have totally reassured her. It's good that she's with Luke. He appreciates how awesome she is. She's completely confident around him now. After the whole crashing his boys' night disaster, Luke calmed Jocelyn. He told her he liked her just the way she is and that she shouldn't try to be anyone else. Jocelyn relaxed after that. It took her a while to trust that she's enough for him. But she finally got there. She realized that if she can't be herself around him, what's the point?

"Hey," Kara says. She's hovering tentatively by the blanket with a supercute boy. "This is Anton."

Jocelyn and I say hey to Anton. Then we just gape at his adorableness.

Anton notices the soccer game. "You think they'll mind if I join?"

"You can totally join," Jocelyn breathes.

"Cool."

I try not to stare too hard as Anton jogs toward the game.

"I didn't know you were coming," Jocelyn tells Kara.

"We weren't sure what we were doing."

"Want to sit?" I ask. We make room for Kara on the blanket.

Seth was crazy when he said I could get Kara and Jocelyn back together. Or I thought he was crazy. Then I thought about it some more on the drive home. If I didn't speak up, was either of them going to?

I called an emergency meeting with Kara and Jocelyn at The Fountain. I wasn't even sure if they'd show up. Jocelyn was the first to arrive. I waved to her from our couch.

"What's this about?" she asked.

"I'm worried that I'll be stuck in the middle of your fight for the rest of the year and we'll graduate and go off to college and then what? You and Kara will never talk to each other again?"

Jocelyn twirled the sash of her wrap dress around her finger.

"New dress?" I asked.

"Yeah. I made it."

"It's gorgeous."

"Thanks. I know this fight is stupid. But we've been mad at each other for so long I don't know how to fix it."

"That's why we're here."

Kara came in and stalked over to the couch. She didn't sit down.

"Ladies," I said, "we need to end this. I can't stand that we're not best friends anymore. I hate that you guys haven't made up yet. Don't you?"

Kara softened. She sat down next to me.

"I'm listening," she said.

That was the start of the end of their fight. We sat on that couch for three hours, talking about everything that had been bothering us. Jocelyn and Kara found their way back to each other. They weren't mad anymore. They were mostly exhausted that the Longest Fight Ever had gone on for so long. All of us wanted to get back to what we had before.

I want us to stay friends forever. But I know that staying friends after we graduate means our friendship has to change. I have to keep hoping that we'll all want to change with it.

"So," I say. "Anton."

Kara nods.

"Is it official?"

"Well, I broke up with Dillon last night, so—"

"You *what*?" Jocelyn says. Kara called me last night after

the breakup, but this is the first Jocelyn's hearing about it.

"We'd been growing apart for a while. We both knew it was coming. But Dillon went ballistic. He kept asking if there was someone else. At first I said it was about how we weren't connecting anymore, but he finally made me admit I was interested in Anton. Then he went off on this tirade about how Anton wanted to break us up all along and I was like, 'We're not breaking up because of him. We're breaking up because of us.' I didn't bother with the whole it's-not-you-it's-me thing. Because it really was both of us."

"I'm so proud of you," Jocelyn says.

"You know what I realized?" Kara says. "Dillon was my Aidan, but Anton is my Big."

We nod contemplatively. *Sex and the City* has vivid moments of clarity. The whole Aidan vs. Big dynamic is one of them. With Aidan, you're getting a fiercely loyal boyfriend who would do anything for you. The boy is an amazing support system and your best friend. Mr. Big is different. He's not as reliable as Aidan. He's not as eager to drop everything and come over to catch that mouse you swear ran under the bed. There will be stomach-churning days of uncertainty with Big. Questions like these will keep you up at night: Does he love me as much as I love him? Will he ever leave me? Why isn't he calling me back? But you tolerate the unknown because what you *do* know is powerful. You connect with Big in a way you never have with anyone else. The chemistry is unreal. Being with Big is what it feels like to be with a soul mate. And soul mates are undeniable.

I'm not sure if Seth is my soul mate anymore. We definitely

had that Big connection. But he's also like Aidan in a lot of ways. It is possible for a boy to be both your best friend and burning desire? Does the complete package really exist? Before Seth and I got in our fight, I would have said yes. But now . . . a lot came out that I didn't know he was thinking. I don't know if he's the person I thought he was.

I hate the distance between us. I hate what it's doing to everything we could become. And I really hate feeling like I don't know Seth anymore.

twenty

Seth

tides have caused the flame to dim

I KNOW I need to get a grip. Stop moping around. Start being my normal self again.

But it's hard.

Why was I so heinous to Skye? I basically accused her of being a conceited snob. It's not her fault she's from money and I'm not.

I wasn't expecting Skye to walk out on me. That was cold. I thought I could trust her. What if I was wrong? What if she walks out every time I tell her something she doesn't want to hear? She might walk out one day and never come back.

Grant comes back to our room from class. He throws a pity glance in my direction. Maybe because ever since Skye left after our fight I've been a miserable wreck. Or maybe because I'm sprawled out on my unmade bed staring at the ceiling when I should be studying. I haven't moved for a long time.

Grant just stands there, staring down at me.

"Take a picture," I grumble. "It lasts longer."

He whips out his phone and snaps a pic.

"You better not post that," I warn.

"Or what? You'll be inspired to get out of bed and act like a member of the human species?"

"No. But I would be inspired to hunt you down and strangle you."

"Dude." Grant surveys my side of the room. "Since when is your side messier than mine?"

He's right. I haven't felt motivated to clean since the fight.

"That's it." Grant walks through the bathroom to Dorian and Tim's room. "Hey, man," I hear him say. "Time for the intervention."

"Game on, bro," Tim says.

Then Tim and Grant are hanging over me like they're visiting some dying relative at the hospital.

"What?" I say.

"This," Tim booms dramatically, "is an intervention."

"Yeah, I heard." I smush a pillow over my face. "I don't need an intervention. I'm fine."

"You are not fine," Grant protests. "Not getting out of bed all day is not fine."

"I got out of bed yesterday."

"For one class. Not good enough."

"I go to the dining hall."

"Barely. Did you even eat today?"

"Whatever, Mom." I yank the pillow off my face. "Food is overrated."

"Can we talk about the real problem here?" Tim says.

"Which is?"

"Um, the fight you're in with Skye?"

"We're not in a fight. We made up."

"Did you? Or did you just start talking again without resolving anything?"

How does Tim know that? I called Skye right after our fight to apologize. She was sorry for what she said, too. That was about it. But when we talk now, it's not the same. Skye was the person I couldn't wait to tell when something awesome happened. Or when something awful happened. She was my best friend. And now it's like . . . we still talk and stuff, but it's not the same. The things we said came between us in a way I don't know how to fix.

There was more bothering her the morning of our fight, though. She was cranky the night before. She was all confrontational, like why didn't I tell her about applying for the internship or changing my major. But I was only trying to protect her. I didn't want her to stress out about some internship I probably won't even get anyway. And it's not like I wasn't listening to her all those times she told me to switch majors. It wasn't until Grant helped me figure out how I could use an art major to actually make a decent living that I was convinced. He went on this twenty-minute diatribe about design, graphics, marketing—every conceivable way to build a successful career with an art major.

"Maybe things aren't exactly resolved," I admit. "We just need time."

"Time for what?" Tim challenges. "Time for Skye to find a new boyfriend who isn't afraid to speak up?"

"I *did* speak up. That's what got me in trouble."

"Skye is perfect for you." Grant says. "We can't watch this. You need to get back to normal."

"How is that possible? Everything I said to her is already out there. I can't take it back."

"But you can explain where it came from. So you have baggage. We all do."

"Yeah, but I've got enough baggage for a bellhop, three U-Hauls, and my dad's truck."

"Then tell her that. Explain who you are. Trust me, she wants to know."

Of course it would take a philosophy major to point out that Skye needs to know more of me in order to understand who I really am. The parts I was showing her weren't enough. If I'm going to trust her with my whole heart, I can't hide the parts I don't like. I have to trust that she'll still love me even with all of my flaws.

"Get up," Tim says. "Fine dining-hall cuisine awaits."

All I want to do is stay in bed and figure out the magic words I need to tell Skye. But I let the guys drag me to the dining hall.

"I am so over make-your-own tacos," Tim complains. "They used to be my favorite dinner. Now I can't stand them."

"The brain is hardwired to absorb habits," Grant says. "It might not have been that you enjoyed tacos per se, but rather your brain was used to going through the motions of expecting and making tacos to allow more energy for deeper thought processes. The concept is closely tied to—"

"Okay, professor, thanks for sharing."

We get seats. The guys dig in. I have no appetite.

A familiar girl's voice says, "Hey, Seth." Then Karen is standing by our table. Smiling down at me like I never broke up with her.

"Hey," I say back.

"Hey, guys."

"Hey," Grant says. Tim nods over a fried chicken leg.

"So," Karen says. "How's it going?"

"Okay."

"I haven't seen you around."

"Yeah, no, I've been . . . busy."

"Oh. Well, I hope things clear up for you. It would be fun to hang out sometime."

How can she do that? Just come up to me like nothing ever happened, like we weren't together, like she didn't get dumped, and say that it would be fun to hang out sometime?

"Uh . . . yeah," I say.

"How are your parents?"

Mom came to visit me after the fight with Skye. She called the next day and didn't like how I sounded. So she drove down to see me. I begged her not to, but there was no stopping her. She took me to a Mexican restaurant off campus for dinner. Being both good and cheap makes it a popular place.

"Please eat something," Mom said. A giant plate of enchiladas sat untouched in front of me.

"I'm not hungry."

"You have to eat."

I glanced around at the other tables. I wasn't in the mood to run into anyone I knew.

Mom took a tortilla chip from the bowl between us. She broke it in half. "I have a new doctor," she said. "He thinks he knows what was wrong with me."

"Really?"

"Apparently, your dad leaving had a psychosomatic effect on me. All of that stomach churning was a symptom of anxiety."

"Why didn't any of those other doctors figure that out?"

"Probably because they only spent about three minutes with me. They didn't ask much about what was going on in my life. They were only focusing on physical issues, not emotional ones."

I couldn't believe Mom had to suffer all that time not knowing what was wrong with her. All because no one took the time to ask.

"The good news is that we know now," she said. "I'm feeling much better."

"That's so good to hear, Mom."

"That's not all." Mom poured me more water from the

pitcher on our table. It had lemons and limes floating on top. "Your dad and I had a long talk. Several long talks, actually."

I sat up straighter. "You did?"

"Yes. He didn't leave because of me. Well, he did, but not for the reasons I thought."

Mom told me that Dad had to take space in order to realize that she's the love of his life. The rink was the one thing that represented their relationship the most. Everything it was when they were young. Everything they were when they first met. The free spirit side of him wanted to be free, to go out and chase that feeling. But Dad realized he was looking in the wrong place. He told Mom he was thinking about moving back home. If she'd have him back. It sounded like she would, but nothing's definite yet. I'm really hoping it works out. The only way for them to get back what they had is to be together.

Now Karen wants to know how my parents are. I can't tell her everything that's gone down since we were together. So I take the wishful thinking route.

"They're excellent," I say.

"I heard you're working at Phantom Fountain. I used to go there all the time. Now we mostly hang out at Le Bus. Do you ever go there?"

"Sometimes."

Grant and Tim are watching this exchange while stuffing their faces. Tim keeps shooting me looks like, *Shut it down!*

"Anyway," Karen says. "Guess I'll see you around."

"Later," Tim shouts. After Karen walks away, he adds, "Much."

"Dude," I say. "I have no interest in Karen. Relax."

"I just don't want your priorities getting confused. Karen is hot."

"Scorching," Grant confirms.

"Who cares how hot she is? I just want to be with Skye."

Skye is obviously the one. We just never see each other. Despite our best efforts, that physical distance has translated into an emotional one.

twenty-one

Skye

crying for the death of your heart

SETH IS beyond stressed over finals. He told me not to come down this weekend. Which sucks because I haven't seen him in forever and things are still weird between us. Last weekend I had to go to this fund-raiser whoop-de-do at my dad's hospital. The weekend before that, Seth had to cover an extra shift at Phantom Fountain. The weeks we've been apart feel like years.

Seth doesn't answer when I call him. I call him again an hour later. He still doesn't answer. I know he's studying like a maniac for finals. But you'd think he'd pick up when he saw that I was the one calling.

What if he's not studying? What if he's not alone?

I call him again half an hour later. Still no answer. The agony of the unanswered phone is the worst.

I have to see him.

He's been working so hard. He's probably freaking out right now even though he's going to kill those exams. I picture Seth lying on the floor of his room, phone suffocated under a pile of Grant's dirty clothes, reduced to a neurotic mess.

He could really use a care package.

True, he said not to come down this weekend. But surprising him with a care package doesn't count. I'll just drive down and give it to him. I won't even stay over if he doesn't want me to. He'll understand that I was concerned about him. I'll put in lots of his favorite treats, like Tastykake Butterscotch Krimpets and Jolly Ranchers and this bag of truffle popcorn I found at the gourmet shop a few days ago. I haven't tried it yet. It's probably not Palomar status, but it's still truffle popcorn.

This whole care package idea is pure serendipity. Jocelyn gave me a beautiful beaded bag for my birthday. The purple box it came in was so cute I had to save it. Now I dig the box out of my closet for Seth. I put some black tissue paper in it so it doesn't look too girly. The bag of truffle popcorn goes in. This rad tape dispenser I was going to give him for his birthday goes in. It looks like an old-school cassette tape and says TAPE DISPENSER where you'd write on the label. I made Seth a friendship bracelet that I was going to give him the next time I saw him. Most of the ones Jade made him last summer have fallen off. I put the friendship bracelet in, too. Now all I have to do is stop at Wawa for the other things on my way down.

I drive through the night to Seth, streetlights whooshing over me, electrified by the need to see him. Not just because I haven't seen him for so long. I have some good news.

I'm going to college in Philly.

At first, Drexel sounded like the best idea. But then I looked into the course descriptions and campus life. I've been getting more and more excited about college. There will be so many campus activities and groups to join and new people to meet. I can't wait to figure out what I want to do with my life. Who I really am. How I'll make the world a better place. And of course I can't wait for the freedom to see Seth as much as I want. But the most important thing is college. I don't want to sacrifice the quality of my education for a boy. Even for a boy I love. Drexel wouldn't have been enough for me. NYU is awesome, but I can't be that far from Seth. I know that things will get so much better for us when we can see each other all the time.

So I decided I'm going to Temple. Not only do they have a strong academic program, they also have lots of activities and community service opportunities. I probably won't see Seth every day, but I'll see him a lot more than I do now.

There's no way I was going to tell Seth all of this on the phone. I can't wait to see his face when he finds out I'll be in Philly next year.

Wawa has everything else I wanted for the care package. I finish packing the box in the parking lot. Then I tie it with a big silver ribbon. My heart pounds as I carry the box to Seth's dorm. I can already feel his lips on mine. I can already see how excited he'll be to hear the good news about next year.

Seth is supposed to come down to sign me in, but the security officer knows me. He lets me go up. Seth doesn't answer when I knock on his door. He probably has his earbuds in. I pound on the door harder. Still no answer. Maybe he went to the library. I'd go look for him there, but you need a Penn ID to get in. University libraries are super strict like that. Sometimes Seth hangs out in his dorm floor lounge. I decide to check there.

As I round the corner to the lounge, I see Seth on the couch. I can tell it's him even from the back. That warm fuzzy feeling I always get when I see him makes my heart pound even faster. But then the rest of the couch comes into view. And I see her.

Sitting with Seth.

Touching his shoulder.

Who is this lounge skank touching my boyfriend's shoulder?

She says something to him. He laughs.

My stomach sinks.

She's probably just some girl from class. They're probably studying for the same final. I'm about to go in and surprise Seth with his care package when the girl on the couch kisses him.

Seth doesn't stop her.

I run out before he can see me.

The image of Seth kissing that girl makes me sick to my stomach. When I get in my car for the long drive back, I already know that image will haunt me forever.

twenty-two

Seth

restless hearts sleep alone

MY BRAIN takes a few seconds to process that Karen is kissing me. One second we're studying. Then we're laughing. Next thing I know, she's all over me.

I pull away from her.

"What's wrong?" she asks.

"What are you doing?"

"What does it look like?"

"You know I have a girlfriend."

"I thought you said it wasn't working out."

"No, it is. It's just ... complicated."

"Well," Karen says, leaning in again. "Let me uncomplicate it."

I jump off the couch. Karen did not just kiss me. That did not just happen.

I did not just let Karen kiss me.

"Where are you going?" she asks.

"We're done." I slap my books and notebooks together. "This can't happen again."

"Okay, relax. I won't kiss you. You don't have to leave."

"Yeah, I do." That one kiss brought everything back. How excited Karen would get when good things happened to me. How she was always so supportive. How passionate she was when we hooked up. Skye used to have that kind of energy. But I haven't felt it from her in a while.

The last thing I want to do is hide anything from Skye. Especially after realizing how important it is to share all the parts of my life with her. Even the parts of which I am not the biggest fan. But if Skye found out about this, she'd think it meant something. Which of course it doesn't.

I can't pretend nothing happened. That would be a lie. Karen kissed me. I pulled away. Only . . . if I'm going to be completely honest, I'd have to admit that I let the kiss go on for a few seconds. That's not something I want to admit to Skye.

How could I have been so stupid?

Back in my room, I attack the canvas on my easel. I smash crushed pigment into the collage of newspaper text plastered all over. The theme used to be generational discontent. Now it's self-hatred.

My phone rings. It's Skye.

"Hey," I answer.

"Hey. What are you doing?"

"Working on a new piece. Well, not really a new piece. Just taking it in a different direction."

"I thought you were studying all weekend."

"I was. I mean, I *am*. I needed a break before my brain exploded."

Silence.

"You still there?" I ask.

"I saw you."

"What?"

"I saw you. With her."

My heart slams against my chest. Skye was here? How is that possible? "What do you . . . You were here?"

"Yeah, I was there. I came to give you a care package. Ironic, huh?"

"But . . . you just left?"

"What would you do if you saw me kissing some other boy?"

"Kill him."

"Then you know how I feel."

"It wasn't like that."

"Really? So you weren't kissing some lounge skank? When you told me not to come down because you were studying all weekend?"

"We *were* studying. She's in my finance class. She kissed me out of nowhere. I shut it down."

"What does that mean?"

"I pulled away from her and left. She knows it can't happen again."

"Why would it happen again? You're not going to hang out with her anymore, are you?"

"No. No, of course not."

"So you weren't kissing her."

"No."

"She was kissing you."

"Yes."

"Out of nowhere."

"Totally. I did *not* see it coming at all."

"Do you like her?"

"No! We just started hanging out again like a week ago. I have no interest in her."

"What do you mean 'hanging out *again*'?"

"We were . . . I knew her last year."

"Who is she?"

Not only did Skye see another girl kissing me, but now I have to tell her that Karen is my ex-girlfriend. I should never have started hanging out with Karen again. I knew she still liked me. How the hell could I have been so stupid?

"That was Karen," I say.

"Karen? As in your *ex-girlfriend* Karen?"

"Yeah. But she knows you're my girlfriend. And she knows I don't have feelings for her anymore. I am so, so sorry."

Silence.

"It won't happen again," I promise. "I won't even talk to her anymore."

"You swear you don't have feelings for her?"

"I swear. I love you. You mean everything to me, Skye."

"Then say you'll come to Sea Bright this summer."

Sea Bright. Nothing but Skye and freedom. I'd give any-thing to go back to what we had last summer, when the only thing that mattered was being together.

Now I have to think about my future. I have to think about where this whole life thing is going and how I'll get there. Switching majors next year won't be easy. I'll be catch-ing up on stuff everyone else has been doing for the past two years. The last thing I want to do is fall even further be-hind than I already am. When I didn't get the internship in Chicago, I assumed it was too late to get one anywhere else. Until Grant helped me come up with an idea. A crazy idea that's a long shot. But if it works, I won't be able to spend the summer with Skye.

"I really want to," I say. "But I don't know if I can yet."

"Why not?"

"There might be a way to get an internship at the Art Institute of Philadelphia."

"I thought you said the deadline passed."

"It did. I'm thinking outside the box on this one." I tell her the idea Grant and I came up with.

"Would something like that actually work?"

"Don't know yet."

Skye sighs into her phone. She's been wanting me to change my major to art ever since she found out I hated business. She knows how important an internship at the Art Institute would be for me. It would open a lot of doors. I'd be exposed to so much over the summer that would make catching up next year way easier. I know she wants me to have this. But she also wants us to spend the summer to-gether. She's been looking forward to our summer all year. I hate that I might not be able to give that to her.

"Well," she says, "I hope you get it."

"Thanks. Look, even if I do get it—which I probably won't because it's such a long shot—that would still give me a week with you in Sea Bright."

"A week."

"I know it's not what we wanted. But it's better than nothing, right?"

Silence.

Skye deserves better than this. She deserves to spend the summer with her soul mate. She deserves a boyfriend who doesn't let his ex-girlfriend kiss him. Someone she can see all the time.

I know I can be the boyfriend she wants. I know I can be better than this.

twenty-three

Skye

one night will remind you

SETH'S SUMMER vacay starting a month before mine was supposed to be a good thing. He was supposed to have time to come up and see me every weekend until I graduated. Then we'd have the whole summer together at the beach if he didn't get the internship.

He got the internship.

Seth worked full-time at Phantom Fountain until it started, so he couldn't take weekends off to visit me. Weekends are the busiest time and he needed the extra tips. His internship is unpaid. He had to save as much as he could to pay rent all summer.

I'm happy for him that he got the internship. It's just so hard to be apart when I was hoping we would be together. I wanted things to get better between us. But then Seth kissed Karen and he's not here with me in Sea Bright and I don't know how everything fell apart. I should be happy right now. I just graduated. I'm going to Temple. Seth and I can see each other a lot more. This was supposed to be the best summer ever.

Except I can't stop crying.

I miss Seth so much. I know we'll be together when college starts. But what if we can't get back the magic we had before? What if the best times for us are in the past?

The worst part is that I don't even know if Seth will be here after his internship ends. He said we'd have a week together. But when his internship started, he found out he could do this workshop at the Art Institute before the fall semester. He could earn a credit toward his new major. Or he could spend a week bumming around the beach with me.

"Enough moping," Jocelyn declares. She and Kara are visiting. I was hoping they wouldn't find me wallowing on the beach like this. I must look even more pathetic than I feel. "Did you not get the memo that Kara and I are leaving tomorrow? We refuse to let you spend our last night in such a tragic state."

"Only happy times allowed," Kara says.

Vague memories of happy times filter through my mind. I used to be a happy person. Back when I thought Seth and I would be together forever. I raced into this thing and fell so hard. Just like I used to zoom out from the carpeted part of the roller rink before I was ready.

"Sorry, guys," I say. "I'm just not feeling it."

"But we always celebrate our last night," Kara pouts. She's right. Every summer when Kara and Jocelyn come visit, we always plan something big for their last night. One time we rented a boat and invited all these random people to our impromptu boat party. Another year we stayed up until sunrise, camping out on the beach and playing the wildest version of Truth or Dare ever. I don't want my misery to bring them down. Which is why I was trying to hide out here while they went into town to do some shopping.

All I can see is Seth kissing Karen. I can't get that nasty kiss to stop replaying on a loop behind my eyes. I know he said he pulled away from her. That it didn't mean anything. But that's not what I saw. He didn't pull away that first second. He let the kiss happen.

Why would he let the kiss happen if he knew we were meant to be together?

My half of the first photo booth pictures we took says it all. Seth making a kissy face in one. Then looking confused in the other.

Jocelyn and Kara sit down on my big beach towel with me. Kara takes her tank top off to reveal a tiny, metallic gold bikini. The way she raved about this bikini when she bought it, you'd think the only reason she visited this summer was to show it off. The boys have clearly appreciated it. Jocelyn looks hot, too. She lost the weight she wanted to this year without any fad dieting. All it took was eating less sugar and working out.

"Seth still might come the week before classes start," Jocelyn reminds me. "I know he really wants to be here with you."

"How do you know?"

"We've seen how he looks at you," Kara says. "The boy is smitten."

"Then why did he kiss his ex-girlfriend?"

"Okay, for the last time: *she* kissed *him*. He has no control over crazy stalker girls randomly throwing themselves at him. The boy is sexy. Girls are noticing. Just like boys are noticing you." Kara tilts her head in the direction of two boys laying out next to us. They've been sneaking looks at me since I got here. Boys usually look at me on the beach. But I don't care. I just want Seth.

"You're both hot," Jocelyn says. "You both get attention. So what? If you both want to be together—which you do—then nothing else matters."

I believe Seth wants to be with me. But he has so much else going on in his life, I feel like I'm not important to him anymore. When we first got together, all we could think about was the next time we'd see each other. I never thought what we had would change. I didn't think it *could* change.

"I'm not sure Seth knows how to be together," I say. "He's still scared of being hurt. I've told him a million times how much I love him. But he keeps holding back. It's like he can't share his life with me completely. Or maybe he just doesn't want to."

"He has to let go," Kara says. "We all have baggage. But at some point, you have to open those bags and confront what's inside. Oh, this is *so* going to be my next topic for A Day in the Life." Kara whips out the mini idea notebook she keeps in her bag. "Anyway. Seth has to drop that garbage he's been lugging around if he wants to keep you."

"Which he totally does," Jocelyn insists. "Don't worry. Right now he's afraid to do the work. But he'll realize you're worth it."

"And if he doesn't?"

"He *will*. I know it."

"The boy has his flaws," Kara says, "but being an idiot is not one of them. Trust me. Next year will be amazing for you guys."

Next year will definitely be amazing for Kara and Jocelyn. Jocelyn is going to Parsons School of Design in New York City. She wants to start her own label. Kara's going to VisArts Boston for filmmaking. None of us knows what's going to happen with our boyfriends. Luke and Anton aren't even going to be near Jocelyn and Kara.

It's weird that we're dealing with all of these changes. If someone told me this would be our lives two years ago, I wouldn't have believed them.

"Come on," Jocelyn says. She gets up and stretches. "We're meeting Adrienne for snowballs. There's a watermelon tangerine one with your name on it."

And a spearmint lemonade one hoping a certain someone visits this summer.

Back in my room later, I'm about to take a shower and get dressed for tonight. The snowball place perked me up. My girls were awesome as always. They convinced me we should drive to Red Bank for some Ms. Pac-Man and pasta. This one Italian place that serves fresh pasta is to die. I guess all these days with no appetite have caught up with me because now I'm starving.

I throw my balcony doors open and step out. There's something about the sound of the ocean from up here that always soothes me. On nights when it's not too hot, I like to sleep with these doors open, the ocean waves drifting me off to sleep. But not even the waves help on nights when I'm missing Seth the most.

Mom is out front in her gardening gear. Most of our neighbors hire landscapers to do their yards. But Mom loves caring for the flowers around our front porch and growing vegetables out back. She said something about planting new azaleas today. I go down to check them out.

"Hi there," Mom says when she sees me on the porch. "Where are the girls?"

"In their rooms getting ready."

"Big night out?"

"We're going to Red Bank for dinner." I flop down on a lounge chair.

"Who's driving?"

"Adrienne."

"Sounds like fun." Mom takes out a trowel from her gardening box. She fluffs the soil in the huge glazed pot that sits at the bottom of the stairs. She always plants the most colorful arrangements in it. "Want to help?"

"I would, but I have to get ready."

"Aren't these azaleas gorgeous?"

"They really are." Mom selected a combination of striped and solid flowers in hot pink, violet, and red. They look beautiful. She makes everything look so perfect. So easy.

"Have you and Dad always had such a good relationship?" I ask, trying to sound casual.

"Pretty much. Better than what most of our friends have, anyway."

"Is it a lot of work?"

"Having a good relationship?"

I nod.

Mom sits on one of the front steps, brushing her gardening

gloves off. "We've had our share of challenges. There will always be challenges in a relationship. The important thing is working as a team to overcome them."

"You make it look so easy."

"It *is* easier with the right person. A good test of a relationship is how well you both deal with challenges. If one person is more invested, it shows. If you're with the wrong person, it feels like too much work. Don't get me wrong—relationships are work. But if you're unhappy more than you're happy, it's not the right relationship for you."

I'm really hoping that Seth is the right boy for me. Despite our problems, I can see glimpses of our future. Like a few nights after I caught Seth in the lounge when I told him about Temple.

"I have some good news," I said.

"Yes, please."

"I'm going to college in Philly."

"You are?" I could hear Seth smiling through the phone. "Where?"

"Temple."

"Good school."

"That's what I hear. I was planning to go to Drexel or Philadelphia University—"

"No, Temple's much better."

"I know."

"That is *awesome*," Seth said. "That is . . . I'm so sorry. I'm an idiot. I swear I'll never let anything like this ever happen again. Please let me make it up to you."

I know in my heart we can make this work. Underneath

the doubt and hurt, there's an unshakable certainty that what we have is something real. Seth swept me away two years ago. I'd been waiting to feel like that forever. But we can't make this work if he doesn't have the same certainty.

Tonight could not be more gorgeous. The air is extra fresh. Tall grass rustles softly in the summer breeze. The sky is crystal clear. I wish Seth were here so much my heart hurts.

Jocelyn, Kara, and I walk down the hill to the beach instead of driving. I see the moon right away. There's a bright point of light next to it that I know is not a star. The moon is a waning crescent. Seth's favorite phase.

"Where are we meeting up with Adrienne?" Kara asks.

"On the boardwalk," I tell her. We're all wearing the delicate sundresses Jocelyn gave us as last-summer-before-college gifts. They flutter around our legs in the warm breeze.

Jocelyn and Kara brainstorm ideas for Kara's A Day in the Life emotional baggage video on the walk down the hill. I'm only half listening. The whole walk down, I watch the moon and hope that everything will be okay.

twenty-four

Seth

can't stand losing you

THE WAY I just randomly noticed my favorite moon phase when I glanced out the window while I was unpacking is a good sign. I remember a night like this, explaining to Skye that what she thought was a star next to the moon was actually Venus.

The fact that I'm still unpacking is ridiculous. I should be done by now. Grant and I have been renting this place for over a month. But between my internship and working nights and weekends at Phantom Fountain, I haven't had much time for home improvement.

I still can't believe I snagged this internship. Our plan was such a long shot. Guess it goes to show that when you have enough passion for something, anything is possible. I was so nervous that day I met with Mr. Ellis. He's the internship director at the Art Institute of Philadelphia. I had to convince him to take me.

"You understand that the deadline has passed," Mr. Ellis told me.

"Yes. I do. And I totally respect that. But I was hoping you would take a look at my portfolio anyway. I would do anything to be here this summer."

He gave me a brief nod. I handed my portfolio to him over the desk. He opened it and began flipping pages. When I shifted in my chair, the leather made a rude noise. I almost blurted out, "It was the chair!" Then I remembered that I was technically an adult.

"Interesting." Mr. Ellis pointed to a print of one of my collages from last year. I called it *Future Tension*. Photos of people crying, screaming, and writhing in pain were plastered all over a plastic top to an end table. "Tell me about it."

"I wanted to translate the anxiety I was feeling about my future into a visual form."

Mr. Ellis studied me. "Why were you feeling anxious about your future?"

"Well, my family sort of scrapes by financially. My dad owned a roller rink, but it went bankrupt. The rink hardly turned a profit on its best days. But it made him happy because it was his dream." I rubbed my hands against my jeans. My dad's failure wasn't what I expected to be discussing at this interview. "Ideally, I'd follow his example to do what makes me happy. I mean, I want to now. I'm switching my major to art next year. Which I should have been majoring in from the start. But I started out as a business major even though I hated it because I was worried about making a decent living. And I wanted to be able to support my mom when she's older. My parents aren't together anymore."

"So you let financial concerns dictate your course of study."

I nodded, embarrassed.

"That's not uncommon. The important thing is that you've gained a sense of clarity, yes?"

"Yes. Totally. All I want to do now is follow my heart. In all aspects of life."

Mr. Ellis smiled faintly. He flipped more pages of my portfolio.

I was literally on the edge of my seat. The chair squeaked when I sat back. I tried to relax. Desperation isn't my most attractive quality.

"I admire your passion," Mr. Ellis said. "You remind me of me at your age."

"I do?"

"You have the hunger. The drive." He closed my portfolio. "Someone who remains a dear friend gave me an opportunity at the start of my career. I want to give you the same chance. You came late to the realization that you belong here. Nevertheless, it's clear that you belong."

"Thank you."

"You'd have to put in extra hours to make up for missing the application deadline. Would that be a problem?"

"No, sir."

"Good." Mr. Ellis stood and extended his hand to me. "We'll be in touch, Mr. Katims."

I walked back to campus in a daze. The next day I got a call saying I was in. Our bootleg plan worked.

It actually *worked*.

This internship has exposed me to a whole new world of emerging career opportunities, like relational aesthetics. It's an area that inspires a dynamic social environment by engaging the audience to actively participate with art. The audience can interact with lights, sounds, buttons, anything that enhances both the artwork and experience of the viewer. More corporations are commissioning this kind of inter-active artwork for their buildings, particularly in lobbies and waiting rooms. I'm excited to explore the possibilities.

The other interns are cool. There are nine of us total. Sometimes we go out after, but I usually have to work. We're all interning in different departments at the Art Institute. I'm in the curator's office. Which is perfect because I'm ac-tually using some skills from my business classes. Every-thing I'm learning about the business side of art has con-vinced me that there are so many exciting things I could do in the art world while still making a decent living. Zero anxiety remains about switching majors. Plus I scored an awesome apartment right where I wanted to live. Grant and I will probably renew our lease for senior year, too.

The phone rings. It's my dad.

"Hey, Dad."

"Hi. How's the internship?"

"Awesome. Even with the extra hours." I was planning to trade some shifts at Phantom Fountain to spend at least one weekend in Sea Bright this summer. But these crazy long days are making it impossible. Some nights I don't even have a chance to talk to Skye. Or we keep missing each other.

"So I have news," Dad says.

"Good or bad?"

"Very good. Your mom and I are getting back together."

"Seriously?"

"Yup. I'm moving back home tomorrow."

What a relief. I've been waiting to hear this ever since the night Mom took me out to dinner and told me what Dad said. But every time Mom or Dad calls, I'm worried one of them changed their mind about getting back together. I'm so happy it all worked out.

"That's awesome," I say. "Congrats."

"We're happy. We knew you would be, too."

Dad does sound happy. After the rink shut down, he got a construction job in Rowayton, Connecticut. He was miserable at first. But he's been healing. I can hear it in his voice every time we talk.

"There's more news," Dad says.

"Good or bad?"

"That depends. How attached are you to the beach house?"

My heart lurches at the mention of Sea Bright. "Not very."

"Good. Because I'm selling it."

"Is it even worth anything?"

"Don't be a wise guy. I've been doing some renovations. She's fixing up nicely."

"You're in Sea Bright?"

"Yeah. I'll be commuting from home until it's done."

I should be there, too. Wanting to be in two places at once is beyond frustrating.

"Are you sad about selling it?" I ask.

"It's time."

Later I'm unpacking a box I "packed" by grabbing a pile of junk off the floor of my closet and dumping it into this box without even looking to see what was in the pile. I take out my old Vans and uncover the playlist I made for Skye after our first summer at the beach. Flashes of endless summer nights wash over me like watercolors.

What am I *doing*? What's more important than us?

I have to go get her.

I can't go yet. But when I can, I'll make sure it's a night she'll never forget.

twenty-five

Skye

you're all my eyes can see

I DRAG myself down the boardwalk slowly, flip-flops scraping against the tattered wood, hardly noticing how gorgeous the ocean looks today. Everything is so tragic. The roller rink has shut down. Its brilliant neon sign has been darkened forever. Part of the boardwalk was damaged in a storm and hasn't been fixed yet. There's this gaping, jagged hole just waiting for someone to fall in. Jocelyn and Kara left. We keep saying we're going to stay BFFs in college. But they'll probably drift away from me along with everyone else.

This summer has no sparkle without Seth.

My heart aches for all the time we could have had together. Not worrying about catching a train or leaving early for the long drive home. Leaving behind school and work and everything else. I keep trying to get over it and move on, but it's so hard to move on from a wish that didn't come true.

The sand-painting guy is out. I know his name is Joe from the sign he has on his collection bucket. Joe always works the concrete strip across from the snowball place that connects the boardwalk to the parking lot. I stop to watch him. A thin ribbon of sand filters from his hand to form precise patterns. He's making a bright pink-and-purple flower.

"Hey," Joe says, squinting up at me against the sun.

"Hey. This one's really pretty." His sand paintings always start with a small design in the center. Then he moves out from there, going around and around in circles to add layers. Every sand painting he does is totally unique. They're usually some kind of flower motif. Or he'll use a shape as a theme. Others are like these intricate spirals that could extend out forever.

"Thanks."

"Do you know what you're going to do before you start?"

"Never. The design comes to me as I go along."

There's something hypnotic about watching Joe work. I love colored sand. It reminds me of the sand birds Adrienne and I made a few years ago at Asbury Park. They started out as tall, thin glass bottles. We used funnels to pour colored sand into them. It was fun to tilt the funnel to change the slopes of the sand. When the bottles were filled with stripes of colored sand, we glued on googly eyes, feathers, and golf tees for beaks to make them birds. Mine still sits on my dresser here at the beach house.

Joe reaches into a bag of aqua sand and grabs a handful. Then he carefully fills in the swirly petals of his flower design by letting the sand filter from his fist.

A couple with two little girls across from me have been watching Joe. One of the girls is enraptured by the sand painting. The other girl is tugging on her mom's hand, begging to go. A boy who looks like he's in college steps up next to me. He smells like mint and Ivory soap. Just like Seth.

I breathe him in and swoon.

It's just too much.

After dinner with my parents, I go over to Adrienne's. Her mom lets me in. I go up to Adrienne's room where she's at her desk. Adele is blasting.

"Did you see Kara's baggage video?" she asks, not looking up from her laptop.

"Yeah. It ruled."

"I know! The girl is a genius. She's going to own film school."

I dive across Adrienne's bed. Her butter-yellow comforter is so soft I could seriously lounge here all day. "Do you think everyone has baggage?"

"Kara thinks so."

"Do you?"

Adrienne turns in her chair to face me. "Yeah, I think so. They have to. Baggage is emotional turmoil that accumulates from painful experiences, right? Who hasn't had at least one painful experience?"

"But aren't some people predisposed to collect baggage?"

"Maybe. Like if they have a hard home life or something."

"So one guy could go through a painful experience . . . say, like, his girlfriend dumping him at graduation or his parents splitting up . . . and he could accumulate way more baggage than another guy would in his exact same situation."

"Hmm." Adrienne comes over and sits next to me. "I wonder why that scenario sounds familiar?"

I hide my face in a pillow.

"Seth has baggage," Adrienne says. "We know this. We also know that boy is seriously in love with you. Baggage is evil. Baggage wants to bring us down. Don't let baggage win."

She's right. Seth might never be able to fully let go of his fear that we won't last. Which just means I have to work harder to show him how much I love him.

Walking home from Adrienne's, something tells me to keep walking down to the beach. It's one of those perfect summer nights. Just like the last night Jocelyn and Kara were here. The full moon is low on the horizon. An orange tinge glows along its edge. The comforting sound of waves crashing softly on the beach calls me down.

I walk along the ocean where the dry sand starts getting wet, carrying my flip-flops. My heart aches like it's going to burst. I want Seth to be here so much it's hard to breathe. But there's one place I can go that will make me feel closer to him.

Our dune is magical. Standing up here looking out at the ocean, it's like the whole world has stopped moving. There is only here. Now. This.

This is where we kissed for the first time. Right here on top of this dune. And now I'm standing here again, waiting for the boy I love to come find me. I have this strong feeling that he'll know I'm here. Which I know sounds crazy. Seth probably won't show up this summer at all. When I talked to him yesterday, it sounded like he was still trying to find a way to visit. It's just . . . the Universe is telling me to be here now. I'm hoping that Seth will be here, too.

I anticipate him in the moonlight.

When I see someone walking toward our dune, I'm not even surprised. I'd recognize him anywhere in his white T-shirt, green cargos, and Vans.

Of course it's Seth.

Of course he's here.

Seth climbs up on the dune. He's carrying a heart-shaped box.

"You're here," he says.

"I was waiting for you."

"I know." He puts the box down. He hugs me tight.

"Don't ever let me go," I whisper.

"Never," he whispers back.

We stay still like that for a while. I press my cheek against his shoulder. He slides his hand down my back. Then Seth takes my face in his hands and looks at me in the moonlight.

"I can't live without you," he says.

Seth kisses me like I've never been kissed before. I can feel how much he loves me, how devoted he is to me, all in that one kiss. It's all I need to know that we're stronger than ever.

twenty-six

Seth

i'll be loving you forever

I DON'T know how I knew Skye would be here on our dune tonight. I just knew.

That's how it is with soul mates. Things happen that you can't explain to anyone else. Sometimes you can't even explain them to yourself. The connection you have defies all logic.

One thing I know for sure is that there's nowhere else I'd rather be than right here with Skye. I can't wait to give her what I made. Plus something else I have for her ... if we can ever stop kissing. I swear I could kiss her forever and it wouldn't be enough.

How is this beautiful girl in love with me? How did I get so lucky?

How could I ever think for one second that anything else was more important than us?

Skye looks over at the box on the sand. "Sorry," she says. "The glitter caught my eye."

"Of course it did." I pick up the box and hold it out to her. "It's a time capsule."

"Seriously?"

"Would I tease about time capsules?"

Skye lifts the lid off the box. I tried to re-create our early days and nights here at Sea Bright by including all of the artifacts I could find. Skee-Ball tickets. A Super Ball we won. Some pink colored sand the sand-painting guy let me have. A sugar packet from the snowball place. My burnt-out glow stick from the beach party where we met. The white rock Skye found on the beach that same night. Plus I put in the mix I made for her after I found that old playlist.

Skye takes out each piece of our history. She's all, "I can't believe you saved this!" and "You remembered that?" I love how everything is making her so excited. Seeing how happy she is makes me want to do more things like this for her.

"Thank you thank you *thank you*!" Skye throws her arms around me. "I can't believe you did all this for me."

"I'd do anything for you. Anything to make you happy." Looking into her impossibly blue eyes, her honey-blonde hair glowing in the moonlight, I don't know how I've managed to be apart from her for so long. Now when I look at Skye, I see my future. A future that feels more secure when I make her feel safe.

There's no doubt in my mind that what I'm about to do next is the right thing.

"I want to give you something else," I say. My heart is pounding. I wasn't expecting to be this nervous. "Everything changed the second I first saw you. You were coming off the boardwalk to the beach . . . and you were the most beautiful girl I'd ever seen. You came out of nowhere and changed my life forever. And the crazy thing is? I didn't even know I was waiting for you."

I reach into my pocket and take out the other box. This one is a lot smaller.

"You're everything to me," I tell her. "You showed me that true love is real. You make me a better person. You make me feel alive. When I'm with you, I feel like anything is possible. Like I can turn my life into whatever I want it to be."

When I open the ring box, Skye's mouth drops open.

"It's a promise ring," I say. "You're the love of my life. You always will be."

Skye puts her hands over her mouth. She's smiling and crying and staring at the ring.

I reach for her left hand. The ring fits perfectly.

"This is really happening," she says.

This love will last. I've never been more certain of anything in my entire life.

Whatever happens next, whatever happens in our future, Skye will always be the one I want to share my life with. She completes all I need to be happy. Our fate is to be together.

I can't wait to see what happens next.

Acknowledgments

THIS BOOK would not have become the best version of itself without the editorial magnificence of Kendra Levin and Regina Hayes. When it comes to polishing a manuscript until it shines, you ladies rule.

The friendly neighbors at Penguin Young Readers Group deserve extra sparkly warm fuzzies. Special thanks to Gina Balsano, Scottie Bowditch, Susan Jeffers Casel, Lisa DeGroff, Felicia Frazier and her sales team, Kristin Gilson, Vanessa Han, Jim Hoover, Anna Jarzab, Eileen Kreit, Jennifer Loja, Draga Malesevic, Elyse Marshall, Linda McCarthy, Shanta Newlin, Janet Pascal, Emily Romero, Kim Ryan, Molly Sardella, Don Weisberg, and Courtney Wood.

Thanks to Elizabeth Eulberg for taking such good care of me, Paula Beisser for a super fun tour of Sea Bright, Kara Doyle and Mami Hasegawa for whipping my butt into shape, and Matt Czuchry for bringing the clarity. Thanks to Gillian MacKenzie and Kirsten Wolf for working it and owning it.

Neesa Peterson of Imperial Woodpecker Sno-Balls and artist Joe Mangrum inspired some of the quirky details I adore in this story. Thank you for sharing your creative energy.

Hugs for the teachers, librarians, booksellers, and other influential grownups who have spread the word to teens about my books. Your support is deeply appreciated.

Ultimate thanks go out to my readers. You motivate me on those days when I need to be pushed. You remind me why I write. And most of all, you inspire me to never give up. Thank you so much for making this life possible. xoxo

Chapter Title Songs

1. The Police, "Bring on the Night," *Reggatta de Blanc*, A&M Records, 1979

2. Foreigner, "Waiting for a Girl Like You," *4*, Atlantic Records, 1981

3. Seals & Crofts, "Summer Breeze," *Summer Breeze*, Warner Bros. Records, 1972

4. Scritti Politti, "Perfect Way," *Cupid & Psyche 85*, Virgin, Warner Bros., 1985

5. Don Henley, "The Boys of Summer," *Building the Perfect Beast*, Geffen, 1984

6. The Rolling Stones, "You Can't Always Get What You Want," *Let It Bleed*, Decca Records, 1969

7. R.E.M., "Get Up," *Green*, Warner Bros. Records, 1988

8. John Mayer, "Something's Missing," *Heavier Things*, Columbia Records, 2003

9. Mat Kearney, "On and On," *City of Black and White*, Aware, Columbia, 2009

10. Steve Winwood, "Higher Love," *Back in the High Life*, Island Records, 1986

11. Richard Marx, "Endless Summer Nights," *Richard Marx*, EMI Manhattan, 1987

12. Sheriff, "When I'm with You," *Sheriff*, Capitol Records, 1982

13. REO Speedwagon, "Take It on the Run," *High Infidelity*, Epic, 1980

14. Bruce Springsteen, "She's the One," *Born to Run*, Columbia Records, 1975

15. Paul Simon, "Crazy Love, Vol. II," *Graceland*, Warner Bros. Records, 1986

16. Bonnie Tyler, "Total Eclipse of the Heart," *Faster Than the Speed of Night*, Columbia Records, 1983

17. Mat Kearney, "Where Do We Go From Here," *Nothing Left to Lose*, Aware, Columbia, 2006

18. The Cure, "Pictures of You," *Disintegration*, Fiction Records, 1989

19. OMD, "If You Leave," *Pretty in Pink* soundtrack, A&M Records, 1986

20. Led Zeppelin, "All My Love," *In Through the Out Door*, Swan Song Records, 1979

21. The Cure, "Pictures of You," *Disintegration*, Fiction Records, 1989

22. Journey, "Faithfully," *Frontiers*, Columbia Records, 1983

23. Journey, "Separate Ways," *Frontiers*, Columbia Records, 1983

24. The Police, "Can't Stand Losing You," *Outlandos d'Amour*, A&M, 1978

25. Foreigner, "Feels Like the First Time," *Foreigner*, Atlantic Records, 1977

26. New Kids on the Block, "I'll Be Loving You Forever," *Hangin' Tough*, Columbia Records, 1988

Turn the page to read
a sample of
Susane Colasanti's next novel

Prologue

205,132,379.

That's how many times his new video has been viewed. That's how many people went to his site, pressed PLAY, and watched the hottest musician in the world perform his latest single.

It wasn't like this a year ago. No one even knew who he was back then. His website only had a few hundred hits. His music wasn't playing on the radio every five minutes. His music wasn't out there at all. And now it's everywhere.

All these girls' eyes on him. All these strangers singing along in their rooms, on the other side of all those screens all over the world.

He's the world's biggest rock star.

He's the boy every girl wants.

He's my boyfriend.

1

When I open my front door, Ethan is holding his phone over his head playing "In Your Eyes."

"Happy anniversary," he says.

"You remembered!" I've been wondering if Ethan was going to remember that our first date was one month ago today. He didn't say anything at school. So I didn't say anything, either. I didn't want to come off like a total spaz over being together for a month. Now I'm so happy I didn't ruin his surprise. I had no idea Ethan was planning this when he said he wanted to come over tonight.

He comes in and kisses me. Still holding his phone over his head. Still playing "In Your Eyes."

"You rule," I tell him.

"I don't rule yet. Maybe I'll rule when we get to where I'm taking you to celebrate. If you like what we're doing."

"You didn't have to do all this."

Ethan hugs me tight. "I wanted to make tonight special."

It's hard to believe we've only been together for one month. It feels like I've known him forever. Today at lunch we were talking about last Saturday night. We were driving around in Ethan's car with no destination in mind. I was supposed to be home in half an hour. But I was desperately trying to block out the harsh reality of time. So was Ethan.

"What if we kept driving?" Ethan said. "Got a motel room in some random town? We could say we got lost."

"And we got the motel room for safety. You were really tired and we were worried you might fall asleep at the wheel."

"Exactly. Your mom would buy that, right?"

"As much as your mom would."

We smirked at each other. Both moms would see right through that scam.

Ethan reached into my lap and held my hand. This was always the worst part of the night, when we knew we'd have to go home soon. I wanted to drive around all night. Holding hands in my lap or his. Singing along to the radio. Getting lost down side streets to make out. We're both shocked by how much alone time we want together. Neither of us has ever felt this way before. Ethan loves having lots of people around. He's a classic extrovert like me. We're both into going out and meeting new people. But nothing compares to how happy I am when it's just the two of us.

A David Bowie song came on. Ethan started laughing.

"What?" I asked.

"Obscure reference."

"Try me."

"'Hey Bowie, do you have one really funky sequined space suit?'"

"*Flight of the Conchords*! I love that show!"

"How are you so awesome?"

"How are *you* so awesome?"

"We're both *Flight of the Conchords* geeks. That makes us both awesome."

"I love our obscure awesomeness."

"I love everything about you."

Ethan made me melt when he said that. I was melting right into the passenger seat. My bones went soft and my heart swelled and I couldn't imagine ever feeling happier than I did right that second. I knew he could see how much I loved him when he looked into my eyes. We haven't said "I love you" to each other yet. But we both know it's there.

That night in Ethan's car feels like it was three weeks ago. But it was only three days ago. When we're together, time dilates and stretches in mysterious ways. It's like we enter our own private universe. Especially when we're alone.

Especially when we're making out.

When Ethan is touching me and kissing me and we're pressed against each other in bed, I never want it to end. I wish we could stay together forever. We usually go to my apartment after school. One minute it'll be three thirty and we'll have three whole hours until Ethan has to be home for dinner. The next thing we know it's after six. How do hours pass in a space of time that feels like minutes?

I suspect time is going to pass even faster tonight. I have no idea where Ethan's taking me to celebrate. But something tells me it's going to be really romantic.

"In Your Eyes" finishes playing. Ethan smiles in that way he has where his eyes sparkle like I'm the most important person to him.

"Are you ready?" he asks.

Why does it seem like he's asking about more than just tonight?

Ethan won't give me any hints in his car. He even takes a few random turns to fake me out. Our small town is already shut down for the night. The river, piers, and boats all seem like they're sleeping. I'm surprised when we end up at his house.

"Didn't see that coming," I say.

"You have no idea."

No one's home at Ethan's house. We go up to his room. Which is filled with candles. Candles in different shapes, sizes, and colors are on every available surface. Candles are on the windowsills, the dresser, the desk, the shelves, the night table. There are even some big pillar candles clustered in a corner on the floor.

Ethan turns the lights off. He starts lighting candles.

"Have a seat," he says. "This might take a while."

I lie back on Ethan's big bed and watch him light the candles. I love watching him. One time he fell asleep in my room. I watched him for almost an hour, memorizing the slope of his nose, the curves of his cheeks, the shape of his lips.

Ethan Cross is the most gorgeous boy I've ever seen. And he picked me.

How did I get so lucky?

After he lights the last candle, Ethan grabs his iPod. He lies down next to me. Then he puts one earbud in my ear and the other in his.

"Thanks again for the song last night," Ethan says. "I loved it."

I was so nervous about sending Ethan "Everything" by Lifehouse. I've had that song on repeat ever since the day Ethan first asked me out. To me, it's Ethan's theme song. It sounds like him. It feels like him. I love losing myself in the sound of him. I'm so deep in the love haze I can't remember what I used to think about before Ethan. Last night I was suddenly inspired to share the song with him. The message I wrote with it said that he's all I want. He's all I need. What we have is amazing.

The second I sent the song, I worried that it was too much. The last thing I want to do is scare him away. But Ethan isn't a typical boy. He doesn't get freaked out by strong emotions. And he's so romantic.

"Your song inspired me to find one for you," Ethan says. Haunting, resonant music starts playing in our earbuds. "Have you heard of Sigur Rós?"

"No."

"They're Icelandic. They have an ambient, post-rock sound." Ethan strokes my cheek. "Their music is beautiful. Just like you."

Melting. On. The bed.

"I don't have the words to tell you how I feel about you. So I found a song in another language to do it for me. I don't know Icelandic, but I read that it's about two people falling in love. How they spend the day together walking around downtown and enjoying being in their own world where they understand each other better than anyone ever has before. It's called 'An Alright Start.'"

"You always out-romantic me. I thought I was being all sweet sending you 'Everything.' You're like, 'I had to go to a whole other language to tell you how I feel!'"

"You were being sweet. You're the sweetest girl I've ever known."

I put my head on Ethan's chest, breathing with him and listening to the music. Ethan slides his fingers through my hair over and over.

"Sterling," Ethan says.

"Yeah?"

"I love you."

I lift my head to look at Ethan. He glows in the candlelight. Just looking at him takes my breath away.

"I love you, too," I tell him.

How could it be any better than this?

2

"**What key is** this in?" Drew asks.

"B-flat," Gage tells him.

"My pages are messed up." Drew makes some notations on his sheet music with a pencil.

"Let's hit it," Stefan says from behind the drums. Stefan is only happy when he's behind the drums.

Drew, Gage, and Stefan are Ethan's band mates. Those guys' high school days are behind them. Now they're working random jobs while waiting for the band to get megafamous. Their band is The Invincibles. Drew plays bass and Gage rocks the keyboard. Along with Ethan's best friend, Miles, these guys are Ethan's closest friends.

The band breaks into "Now and Forever." Ethan's hoping it will be their first single. He looks at me while he sings.

Don't worry about tomorrow.
We always have today.

Right now is all that matters.
Right now is here to stay.

Ethan wrote this song for me. I couldn't believe he wrote it in two days. He said he was inspired by his muse (i.e. me). "Now and Forever" is all about appreciating the moment you're in, anytime, anywhere. It's about quieting the noisy part of your brain that's anxious about the future and soothing it by finding happiness in whatever you're doing right now. Ethan said that I make him happier than he's ever been. He wanted to write a song that would capture how happy he felt with me.

Yeah. My life is pretty good.

I put my feet up on the edge of the couch cushion, hugging my knees to my chest. Ethan snagged this couch for the garage when his parents redecorated the den. It's perfect for watching band practice.

"That was awesome," Ethan tells the guys when the song ends.

"Did you see 'Aluminum Rain'?" Gage asks Ethan. "I sent it to you last night."

Ethan nods.

"Can we try it?"

Things always get awkward when Gage wants The

Invincibles to play a song he wrote. Everything the band plays was written by Ethan. There's an unspoken understanding that Ethan's music is phenomenal. That's why Ethan is destined to be a rock star.

But Gage thinks he's also destined to be a rock star, despite his music lacking the depth and soul of Ethan's. That's why he keeps pushing Ethan to add his songs to the set list. They've already done some shows at local venues. So far, Ethan's songs are the only ones they've played.

"We don't really have time," Ethan tells Gage.

"Then can we at least add it to the next set list?"

"I don't think that would be the best approach," Ethan says.

"Seriously? Are we ever going to play my songs?"

Ethan glances at the other guys. Drew picks at his bass uncomfortably. Stefan itches to pound the drums.

Gage faces Drew. "You liked 'Aluminum Rain.' You said it spoke to you."

"It's a good song," Drew agrees.

"But not as good as Ethan's songs. Right?"

Drew throws Stefan a look. Stefan looks at his drums.

"Come on, man," Drew says. "Take it easy."

"No, I want to know. That's what you guys really think, right? That Ethan's songs are better than mine. Why don't you just admit it so we can move on?"

"Your songs are good," Stefan says. "Maybe just not as . . . strong."

"We all want to be successful," Drew says. "That's only

going to happen if we rock our strongest sound. You know how hard it is to get people's attention. How long have we been practicing in this garage? Two years? And we only started playing gigs . . . what, three months ago? Things are finally happening for us. We have to stick with what's working."

"You're right." Gage yanks the cover over his keyboard. He grabs his bag.

"Where are you going?" Ethan says. "We still have twenty minutes."

"I'm done."

"You mean . . . for today, or . . . ?"

"I'm not sure this is working for me anymore."

"Dude," Stefan says. "Don't be such a drama queen."

Gage turns to Stefan like he's going to say something. Then he stalks out of the garage to his car. He slams his door and peels out.

"Was it something I said?" Stefan wonders.

Watching band practice is usually fun. These four guys all started out at the same level, practicing in Ethan's garage three days a week after school. The thing is, they're not going to be at the same level for much longer. Especially now that Zeke is in the picture.

Zeke Goldstein is a beast.

Ethan met him at a show they played in New Haven. Zeke wasn't even there scoping out talent. He was on a blind date his friend set up. As soon as Ethan sang his first note, Zeke knew he was destined for greatness. He was determined to sign Ethan right away. Zeke is on the grind 24/7. He just started working on building Ethan's career and Ethan already has thousands of followers. He says Ethan is about to go places beyond his wildest dreams. And that boy's dreams are pretty wild.

Zeke will be the first one to tell you that he discovered Ethan and that he deserves to take credit for Ethan's future success. Which comes off as arrogant to me. The way Zeke sees it, he's confident in his ability to build an artist's career. And he believes in Ethan more than anyone he's ever represented. He even dropped a few clients to make more room for Ethan on his list. Zeke insists Ethan's career is about to blow up.

"I guess we're done here," Ethan says.

Drew packs his bass. Stefan riffs on the drums.

Ethan comes over and scrunches against me on the couch. "Sorry about the drama," he says.

"Honey badger don't care."

"It just takes what it wants."

"And of course what does the honey badger have to eat for the next two weeks?"

"Cobra!" we both yell.

We were on the floor the first time we saw that video. I don't know what's so hysterical about it. But we were dying. We were also dying over that video of the race car. The race car isn't even moving. It's just a picture of a race car. Some guy is making race-car sound effects over it like, *"Rinnnng neee neee nee nee neeeee!"* Again, way more hysterical than it should be.

Ethan scrunches even closer to me. He holds me tight.

"I have to get up," he says. "But I don't want to get up."

"I don't want you to stop hugging me."

"They need to invent a tool to pry us apart."

He's right. It's like we have to touch each other all the time or we'll die or something. "They should call it the peeler-offer."

"OXO should make one."

"I was just going to say that!" OXO is one of my favorite brands of kitchen tools. They're into form plus function. Which is the best combo for cooking supplies.

Drew and Stefan shuffle over to talk to Ethan before they leave. I go inside. The last thing I want to be is the lead singer's clingy girlfriend.

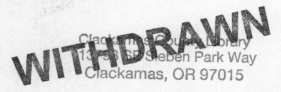